David Allan Evans grew up in Sioux City, Iowa. He began college on a football scholarship, and by the time he graduated—majoring in English and minoring in Biology—he was writing poetry and fiction. His interest in literature and natural history began in his teens when his self-educated father recited Shakespeare and spoke often of Darwin and other great observers of animals. The author of nine collections of poems, he was a professor of English and writer in residence at South Dakota State University for many years, as well as a Fulbright Scholar, twice in China, and poet laureate of South Dakota for 14 years.

For Jan, and for Shelly, David, and Kari

David Allan Evans

THE MAZE

A Fable

AUSTIN MACAULEY PUBLISHERS™
LONDON • CAMBRIDGE • NEW YORK • SHARJAH

Ordering Information
Quantity sales: Special discounts are available on quantity purchases by corporations, associations, and others. For details, contact the publisher at the address below.

Publisher's Cataloging-in-Publication data
Evans, David Allan
The Maze

ISBN 9781645756477 (Paperback)
ISBN 9781645756484 (Hardback)
ISBN 9781645756491 (ePub e-book)

Library of Congress Control Number: 2020909871

www.austinmacauley.com/us

First Published (2020)
Austin Macauley Publishers LLC
40 Wall Street, 28th Floor
New York, NY 10005
USA

mail-usa@austinmacauley.com
+1 (646) 5125767

Table of Contents

1: Once Upon a Time 11

2: Announcements 23

3: Uniqueness 26

4: A Letter from the Possums 34

5: Morning Maneuvers 39

6: A Difference of Opinion 44

7: Dream of the Week 48

8: A Collaboration 50

9: The Maze 53

10: Learning the Way 55

11: Opening Day 61

12: One Mad Squirrel 65

13: Grandpa Possum Tells a Story 68

14: Number Three's Secrets 73

15: Maze Momentum 81

16: Prove It 88

17: "Closed for Repairs" 93

18: Respect vs. Affection 95

19: The Dream Machine 100

20: Two Lives 106

21: The Kingdom of Sharing 112

22: What Is a Sniff? 126

23: Delayed Response 132

24: Temptation 138

25: First Therapy Session 144

26: Claws Gets a Second Opinion 151

27: Yes Yes Yes 153

28: Report from The Crow 155

29: Second Therapy Session 160

30: To Leap or Not to Leap 165

31: Between Friends 168

32: What If? 173

33: Stub Rats on Sniff 177

34: Enter the Serpent 183

35: New Woods' Election Notice 187

36: Owl's Last Appearance; the Election 188

37: Coda: At the Edge of The Meadow 197

1: Once Upon a Time

Once upon a time, a famous old owl lived in a huge oak tree in the center of The Woods. His name was Owl, and he was the leader of all of the animals. In his younger years, he had been not only a great hunter but a superb athlete of the air. He was exceptionally agile—the most agile flier of all—and could swoop through the night without making the slightest sound. If a mouse could have heard him coming (and no mouse could) it would have heard something like the sound of the tiniest feather from the tiniest wren, falling.

And Owl was said to be rich. During his years as leader he had been signing autographs for a fee, and appearing at weekly events, called Appearances, that celebrated his greatness. These events, which took place every Friday evening after work, had become, over time, public meetings, attracting animals from all over The Woods. Recently, however, the old leader had announced his retirement. He would make only three more Appearances—the final one on election day, when a new leader will be chosen—and then fly away into retirement.

Though most of the animals were talkers, Owl's words were few in number. And yet he was considered wise. "A quiet beak, a wise head" was a saying widely heard in The Woods. Another saying was: "Without words, a lightning bug's flash says *I am here*; without words, Owl's flight says *I am not here*."

Because Owl was so popular, most of the animals had an opinion about his quietness in flight, or terseness as a speaker.

There was a hawk named Wing, an imposing, powerful flier who made a lucrative living as a writer, known mostly for his poetry. Wing had a ceaseless curiosity about all kinds of subjects: science, philosophy, and psychology, for instance. And he had plenty of opinions—often contrary to the daily drift of conversation in The Woods—which he never hesitated to express. He appreciated Owl's graceful and silent flying, but regarding his terseness, he was known to have said, "Why should an owl or any animal speak if it has so little to say?"

Wing's best friend was a butterfly named Butterfly, an advanced student of science and philosophy. Like Wing, she was very curious about life in The Woods, and spent much of her time observing, and formulating ideas and theories based on her observations. She would fly around in a seemingly erratic way, as if constantly wafted by a breeze, or perch on a branch, to read and/or make notes. Butterfly enjoyed her quick-flitting, ubiquitous life. Her opinion of Owl's terseness was based on logic: since he was admired for his silence as a hunter, he assumed that he'd be admired for his silence in other matters.

A large, young, athletic, ambitious red squirrel named Claws lived in the highest branches of The Oak. At times bold, and at times diffident and naive, Claws was a mail carrier, and an aspiring poet. As to his opinion of his famous leader, he believed that because Owl had perfected at least one thing in his life—his silent flying—he deserved to be famous.

The best athlete of The Five—a pack of rat deputies—was Number Three, who would become a teacher and athletic trainer. He was quite independent, though also congenial and sociable, and had a strong need to excel and to encourage excellence in others. Number One was the head-rat of the pack, Number Two was an effective phrase-maker and announcer, and Number Four would become a part-time psychologist. All of The Five had a very favorable opinion of Owl.

The commander of The Five was Sniff, a thinly-built rat with a high-pitched, shrill voice and a habit of sniffing while talking to others (hence his name). Living beneath the spreading roots of The Oak, he was intelligent, self-assured, highly ambitious, and, after Owl, the most popular animal in The Woods. According to a well-known rumor, he had once been injured in a fight with a notorious fox. Sniff made his living as Owl's spokes-rat, accountant, banker, business partner, speechwriter and speech coach. His overall opinion of Owl's quietness and terseness was, understandably, very favorable.

Stub, a mole named for his stubby tail, was Sniff's assistant. He was a very serious animal, a good worker, and had a vivid imagination. There was no reason for Stub not to have a positive opinion of Owl.

There was a chubby spider named Spider, an architect whose intricate web designs were widely admired. She liked to compare Owl's silence in the air to a spider's silent launching of filaments to start a web. For her, Owl was a master of what she called the "architecture of flight." As for Owl's terseness, Spider assumed that it was simply the result of a limited vocabulary.

Only 34 to 36 rabbit hops from The Oak, and close to The Meadow, there was The Pond, where a bullfrog named Frog lived. An instructor of bug-catching, Frog spent half of his life in the water and half on the bank, and so he had a double point of view about almost everything.

When one day he was asked, "What do you think of Owl's silence as a flier?" Frog replied: "Good/bad."

"Why is it good?" asked the questioner.

"Because being soundless enables him to survive easily as a hunter," said Frog.

"And why is it bad?" asked the questioner.

"Because his prey can't hear him coming, and so is easily trapped in his sharp talons, and eaten."

A very long rat snake called Snake, who was said to make a living from shady dealings, probably wouldn't have cared enough to have an opinion about Owl. The Crow, a brain scientist from The Isle of Crows, had once lived in The Woods and had been one of Owl's friends. Grandma and Grandpa Possum, who were retired, thought very highly of Owl.

Fox (the one who had had the fight with Sniff) lived at the edge of The Woods. It was said by many that he didn't have or need a job. Very few of the animals, if any, dared to get close enough to Fox to ask him what *he* thought of Owl.

Regardless of one's opinion of the famous leader, there was one fact about him on which all of the animals agreed:

though his aging wings had begun to clatter slightly, and he had begun to repeat himself, and could no longer swivel his head completely around on his majestic shoulders, he was still known as The Woods' most distinguished embodiment of The Great Tradition of Wings.

It was an early Friday evening in the fall. A good-sized crowd—essentially the same one week after week—had gathered at The Oak for an Appearance. The first item of business was the collection. This evening the money would go to the Owl Retirement Fund. The Five moved through the crowd quickly with their collection cups. When they were finished, Number One took the money to The Hole, Owl's home in The Oak.

After several more minutes, Owl stepped out of The Hole and was standing on The Big Limb, with his microphone, ready to speak to the applauding crowd below. In a rigid row in front, like sentries, stood The Five, their teeth showing. There were many other rats too, along with raccoons, porcupines, minks, frogs, sparrows, turtle doves in nearby trees, and a small flock of blackbirds hovering in the air over The Oak. Claws, Spider, Stub, Frog and the Possums were there too, as usual. Butterfly and Wing were perched, as was their habit, next to each other on a branch at beak-level with Owl. Sniff was just inside The Hole, waiting for his turn to talk.

The applause subsided and stopped. Owl tapped on his microphone with a claw to make sure it was turned on, and raised his free wing in a graceful gesture.

"My fellow animals," he said, "I have much gratitooooooooood—much gratitoooooooooood—for your beeooooooooootiful kindness—your beeooooooooootiful kindness—during all of my years of leadership. It is yoooooooooo who have shown great fortitoooooooooood in your doooooooooootiful efforts against Fox. It is yoooooooooo—it is yoooooooooo—who have kept us from great danger. It is yoooooooooo who have saved us."

The Five began to stamp their feet in unison, saying in perfect harmony: "Dooooooooooty, dooooooooooty, dooooooooooty." There was much applause and shouting and whistling.

Owl raised his free wing again, and the noise and stamping subsided. He set the microphone down on the limb. Then, just as silence came over the animals, he blinked, swiveled his distinguished head—stiffly—three quarters around, then back, blinked again, took his famous three steps outward on The Big Limb, where he paused. He did not spring from the limb; he was too old for springing. Instead, he simply stepped off into the air, fell straight down like a big white stone and then suddenly, just as the ground was about to meet him, opened his wings and swooped grandly over the heads of the animals—who felt the warm, familiar wash of wings and heard their slight clattering—then rose and circled the crowd once, twice, swooped low once more, nearly touching the ground with a wide wing, then disappeared into the trees.

During Owl's grand disappearance, in the midst of the loud cheering, Sniff had stepped out onto The Big Limb and picked up the microphone. All eyes were on him as he waved to the crowd graciously, as if the left-over cheering for Owl was not meant for Owl, but for himself. When the cheering and shouting subsided, he began to talk.

"Thank you. Thank you," he said in his shrill voice. He waited until all was quiet, and went on: "My fellow animals of The Woods, today we are gathered to discuss two important matters. At this meeting, we intend to kill two birds with one acorn, so to say." Then he smiled and sniffed.

Wing yelled abruptly, "There you go again, knocking the birds, as usual!" He then left his perch and flew to a branch close to where Sniff was standing on The Big Limb, so he wouldn't have to yell and could address not only Sniff but the crowd.

Sniff paused, and smiled. "Oh," he said, "we're sorry if we offend anyone with our words, especially our po-etic friend with wings."

"Friend?" said Wing.

"Now, let us continue," said Sniff. "The first matter we want to address is the matter of tradition."

"You mean 'The Tradition of Wings'?" said Wing.

"I mean 'The Tradition,'" said Sniff.

"Why not call it what it really is—'The Tradition of Wings'?" said Wing.

Sniff smiled again and went on: "All of us know and appreciate the long and distinguished leadership of Owl, a great athlete—of the air, that is. We need to honor him; we need to honor his greatness. But we must also realize that he is old and will be retiring soon, in fact, after his last Appearance, which will take place—as you all know—two weeks from today. What is important, when we decide to choose a new leader, is that we maintain the great tradition that Owl has so wonderfully stood for.”

“You mean, of course, The Tradition of Wings,” said Wing.

“With this in mind,” said Sniff, ignoring his detractor by looking away, “we need to consider ways of carrying on The Tradition. We need to find an appropriate way to celebrate and perpetuate The Tradition. In fact, my fellow animals of The Woods, I have good news to report to you this evening.”

Again, there was applause and cheering. Sniff lowered the microphone to his side, and waited until the noise died down, then raised the microphone to his whiskers: “We’ve already got a plan for carrying on The Tradition,” he said. “All of you will be extremely happy with the plan.”

“Oh sure,” Wing said. “You’ve got a plan alright—for you and your fellow rats.” It was too late for Wing’s words to have any effect, since the applause and cheering had risen again, and once again, Sniff waited until it subsided. Then he went on: “For now, please trust us that the legacy of Owl will be carried forward after his retirement. For now, trust that our plan will be exactly what is needed to keep The Tradition alive—forever!”

There was more cheering, more applause. When it subsided, Sniff said, “And now, my fellow animals—let us turn to the second matter of this important Appearance, a matter which is related to the first one, The Tradition. I am referring to the ranking system.”

“I’ve been looking forward to this one too,” said Wing, nodding, and then cocking his head. Sniff ignored Wing and kept on speaking. “We have given this topic much consideration in the past few weeks. We have consulted with the Ranking Committee, the Committee on Status, and the Committee on General Matters of Animal Reputation."

"Excuse me," said Wing, "but don't all of these committees deal with the same topic?"

"Oh," said Sniff, "but our distinguished po-et with wings surely misunderstands us. The truth is that standing and status are very complicated matters. Obviously, we need several committees to handle such complicated and important matters. But let us continue." He waved his paw at Wing, and continued: "My fellow animals, the collective decision of our three distinguished committees is that our former ranking system is out of date, and that another system, which is more appropriate, should take its place."

"Here we go again," said Wing. "All for the rats." At this point—after sniffing, and smiling—Sniff began to ignore Wing completely, raising his high-pitched voice to an urgent level. "In former times, ranking animals was a haphazard and inefficient practice, as well as one which favored wings, and I am here today to announce to you all, that a new ranking system has been established, a ranking system that is altogether fair." Sniff paused, allowing for some applause and cheering, which was mostly from the rats. Then all of the animals became silent. "This new ranking system will be utterly fair and just, and furthermore, it will be a system that is expedient and efficient and easily implemented and easily enforced."

"And just what is your so-called new, so-called system?" said Wing.

Sniff smiled. "In the new system," he said, "rank will be based on athletic ability, of course, and self-sacrifice. Only as a group can we defeat Fox. But rank will furthermore be based on teeth—I mean teeth that are used mostly for gnawing—as well as having four legs, and a thin tail, and, in order to honor the great Owl, as I said before, superior athletic ability. All animals with those great qualities shall be considered leaders, and all the other animals shall be considered followers."

There was applause and cheering again, especially from the rats. Several squirrels looked puzzled—some began to swish their tails—while The Five were stamping their feet. Most of the birds in the trees and in the air were not cheering.

"You see," Sniff said, breaking in just as the noise was subsiding, "it's a simple system. But let me explain fur—"

"There you go again," Wing said. "All for your own kind—was I right?"

"And now, you may ask, 'Why are teeth so important?'" said Sniff.

"Yes, I may ask," said Wing, shifting his position on the branch.

"Must we remind you of our great enemy, Fox? Must we remind you today of the countless animals killed randomly and violently by Fox? And what good, may I ask, are wings against this terrible foe?" asked Sniff.

"Show us the evidence that Fox is killing at a higher rate these days than ever before," said Wing. "What proof, what facts do you have?"

"Let me tell you," said Sniff, looking not at Wing but at the crowd. "Teeth are of the first importance. If it weren't for these teeth (Sniff paused to show his teeth as if giving the crowd a mock smile) there would be no survival. If it weren't for these teeth, The Woods would not be The Woods."

"What about talons and beaks?" asked Wing. "Are you saying they're not important?"

"But our distinguished po-et with wings misunderstands us," said Sniff. "Let us explain. You see, all animals are important—all animals are needed—except Fox, that is. It's just that some animals are leaders and some are followers."

"You just said that all animals are important," said Wing. "But you don't believe that. You're faking it again. You're all for the rats and the rats only. And besides, what makes you think you're the one to decide which animals are important or less important, or which ones are leaders and which ones are followers?"

"We need to destroy Fox before he destroys us," said Sniff. "And we have devised a new ranking system that will accomplish this mission. *We* will win, in the end." For the first time during the Appearance, Sniff stared at Wing, and spoke with force: "*We* will win, in the end," he said again, and his look became a scowl.

"We'll see about that," said Wing.

"We will destroy Fox," said Sniff, "and then we will establish a new kingdom."

"Yeah, sure," said Wing. "A new kingdom of rats." Just after the word "rats" left his beak, Wing and Butterfly were in the air and flying away, followed closely by many of the other birds. A few squirrels left their low limbs and climbed straight up.

Sniff raised his paw; the applause resounded. The Five were stamping their feet, and the noise of the four-legged animals, especially the rats, filled The Woods.

Now Sniff was finished. He graciously acknowledged the crowd with a smile, and slipped back inside The Hole. A few minutes later, after the noise died, the crowd dispersed.

2: Announcements

Just before sunrise the next morning, Sniff and Number Two, who was holding a microphone, were standing on The Big Limb. Number Two was about to send messages to all corners of The Woods.

"HEAR ME, HEAR ME: MESSAGES OF THE DAY!" he announced loudly. And then, after a brief pause, he repeated, "HEAR ME, HEAR ME: MESSAGES OF THE DAY!" He paused briefly, then went on, announcing his new batch of sayings, in pairs, as was his habit.

OLD WOODS DEAD!
NEW WOODS AHEAD!
OLD WOODS DEAD!
NEW WOODS AHEAD!

OLD WOODS WRONG!
NEW WOODS STRONG!
OLD WOODS WRONG!
NEW WOODS STRONG!

WINGS ARE FOR BLEEDERS!
TEETH ARE FOR LEADERS!

WINGS ARE FOR BLEEDERS!
TEETH ARE FOR LEADERS!

UP, UP AND AWAY
NEVER SAVES THE DAY!
UP, UP AND AWAY
NEVER SAVES THE DAY!

WINGS FLY AWAY,
TEETH SAVE THE DAY!
WINGS FLY AWAY,
TEETH SAVE THE DAY!

"Alright," said Sniff, "Now let's hear some one-liners."

"Yeah sir," said Number Two, and he began again, repeating each message:

WINGS ARE FOR BIRD BRAINS!
WINGS ARE FOR BIRD BRAINS!

SAYING SO, MAKES IT SO!
SAYING SO, MAKES IT SO!

DO A GOOD DEED TODAY!
DO A GOOD DEED TODAY!

"Or else," said Sniff.

"Or else what, sir?" asked Number Two, with a perplexed look.

"Do a good deed today, or else," said Sniff.

"Whatever you say, sir," said Number Two, and then announced:

DO A GOOD DEED TODAY! OR ELSE.

"No, idiot," said Sniff, "come down hard on the 'or else.' Say it like you mean it."

"Yeah, sir, I got it," said Number Two, and shouted as loud as he could:

DO A GOOD DEED TODAY—OR ELSE!

DO A GOOD DEED TODAY—OR ELSE!

"That's better," said Sniff. Now it was his turn. He took the microphone from Number Two, and raised it to his whiskers and shouted in his high-pitched, shrill voice, "WEEEEEEEEEEEEEEEEEEE!" He paused, waiting for a reply, which was immediate and intense, though lacking the mechanical intensity of his own voice in the microphone: "IIIIIIIIIIIIIIIIIIIIIIIIIIIIIIIIIIIIIIII!" It was a sound of a voice high over The Woods, a voice from the sky.

Sniff responded immediately: "WEEEEEEEEEEEEEEEEEEEEEE!"

The reply came again, louder this time, "IIIIIIIIIIIIIIIIIIIIIIIIIIIIIIIIIIIIIIII!"

3: Uniqueness

The source of the far-away response to Sniff's call was Wing, flying over The Meadow. He was hunting, and also thinking about some lines toward a new poem, and still agitated because of Sniff's speech the day before.

When he spotted a young rabbit sitting close to her hole, he made a friendly landing on a low branch of a young ash tree nearby, leaving plenty of room between himself and her. To feel safer, however, she moved closer to her hole; yet even though she felt somewhat apprehensive, she was also curious enough to start a conversation, knowing that Wing was famous.

"What's it like being a poet?" she said.

Wing was glad to be recognized and to get the question, since it was rare for him to get such questions, and he always enjoyed talking about poetry. "To be a poet," he replied, "means that you must always be trying to make poems; it means that you are never not interested in making poems. Everything you see, do and feel counts in some way toward the making of poems. Nothing you observe or do should slip past your awareness, because it might fit into a poem, if not today, someday."

"Can you give me an example?" asked the rabbit.

"Take our conversation right now," said Wing. "The way you're sitting there on your haunches, the way your long, pink ears are perked up; the thin reddish veins in them; the way you ask questions, your eyes lighting up when you're curious. Everything you think and do and say and everything I think and do and say, right now, at this second, can be part of a poem."

"But that doesn't sound like stuff you'd put in a poem," said the rabbit. "That sounds pretty normal to me."

"It may be normal to you, and it may even be normal to me," said Wing. "But everything is possible when poetry is involved." Now that he had a good listener, Wing became animated; his grip on the limb loosened somewhat, and he went on.

"Consider your long ears, for instance," he said. "If I wanted to make a poem about a rabbit, I might start with the long ears, which I've seen many times, just as I can see your ears right now, as we're talking. Now you take Stub, a mole I know. He doesn't have long ears; in fact, his ears are not even visible. He can hear alright, and see what he needs to see, but mostly he *feels* his way through life, through the dirt that nobody can see into. Stub is a digger, so he needs good claws and a good touch so he can feel the dirt and dig, dig, dig, dig, dig through it. If I wrote a poem about Stub I would consider, for sure, the fact that he's a digger. He doesn't need your long ears, swift long legs, or even good eyesight. But what he needs he *has*, in abundance. He gets along fine with what he has."

"That makes some sense," said the rabbit. "Now tell me about me. If you made a poem about me, how would you make it?"

"It all depends," said Wing, realizing that he had said something vague. "If I made a poem about you I might begin it with a line like: 'Long ears aim up-wind.'"

"You would start with my ears?" said the rabbit.

"I wouldn't *need* to start with your ears," said Wing. "There isn't a rule saying I *have* to do that. It's just that your long ears set you apart from other animals. Without long ears, you wouldn't live as well as you live."

"What do you mean I wouldn't live as well?" asked the rabbit.

"I mean that your ears make it possible for you to go on living," said Wing, "to go on getting food and avoiding trouble."

"But I'm a fast runner too, and a good zig-zagger—nobody can catch me," said the rabbit.

"Yes, for sure," said Wing. "Your long legs are important too, and your keen eyesight. But lots of other animals have long, fast legs and keen eyesight. And yet you also have long ears. You are unique with your long ears."

"I'm unique?" said the rabbit. "What does unique mean?"

"It means special. You're a special animal. No other animal is quite like you. Some may have certain abilities you have, but none have all of your abilities. Only you have all of your abilities."

"So, if you made a poem about me, you would say I was unique. Is that right?"

"Yes, I would say you are unique."

"Thank you," she said.

"You're welcome," he said. A sparrow flew over and the rabbit's ears perked up.

"But what about Fox?" she asked. When she said the word "Fox," her voice quivered slightly.

"What *about* Fox?" asked Wing.

"How could you make a poem up about Fox and call *him* unique?" she said.

"Fox *is* unique," said Wing. "He's no different in his uniqueness."

"But Fox is bad; he'd eat me if he ever caught me," said the rabbit.

"Yes, I know he would, and he could eat me too if he ever caught me," said Wing. "But that doesn't mean he's not unique."

"What's unique about Fox?" asked the rabbit.

"Have you noticed how he moves?" asked Wing.

"Me, notice how Fox moves?" said the rabbit. "You've got to be out of your mind. How could I notice how he moves when I'm running from him to get away? All I need is a glimpse of red and I'm lickety-split gone."

"Okay, I understand," said Wing. "But I have noticed how Fox moves. I've watched him for hours. He moves about as if he's wandering; his head goes one way and then another, looking around for anything that might get his attention. He looks as if he's just wandering, with nothing to do, but really, he's looking for something to chase or surprise. Anything that's moving, anything alive is interesting to him. His so-called wandering, I mean, is deliberate. It's what keeps him alive."

"That scares me, just to hear you say it," said the rabbit, who started leaning toward her hole.

"Well, that's what Fox is," said Wing, relaxing his grip on the branch, and speaking a bit slower and more casually. "He's a deliberate wanderer with sharp eyes. And a sharp nose."

"And deadly teeth, too," said the rabbit.

"Yes, that's true," said Wing. "But he's a wanderer, first; he must discover his food, which is very wary of him, and then he runs after it."

"Wary? What does that mean?" asked the rabbit.

"It means being alert, aware," said Wing.

"Well, I'm wary too," said the rabbit.

"I know you are," said Wing. "But there's a difference between being the hunter and being the hunted. Hunters are always looking one way, ahead of them, and the hunted are always looking at both what is in front of them and what is behind them."

"Especially what's behind them," said the rabbit.

"For sure," said Wing, who was thinking that the distinction he just made would make a good poem. Both he and the rabbit were quite relaxed now, as they talked.

"If you made up a poem about me," said the rabbit, "how would you begin?"

"As a matter of fact," said Wing, "I do have a beginning line."

"Tell me it," said the rabbit. She cocked her long ears.

"I already did."

"You already did?"

"'Long ears aim up-wind," said Wing, enunciating each word slowly, and carefully.

"That's it?" said the rabbit.

"That's it," said Wing.

"Do you have any more lines?"

"My second line might be something like: 'Winter's sun is frozen in her eye.'"

"Frozen in my eye? What does that mean?"

"I mean," said Wing, "that when I watch you, sitting still in the meadow, in winter, with your ears perked up and aimed up-wind so you can hear any possible danger in that direction, that your eyes look frozen. You're very still—so a hunter like Fox can't see you—and your eyes are very still. They look frozen, and the sun is reflected in them. And the sun is round like an eye too, and in winter it looks sort of frozen like everything else, and—"

"And what else?" asked the rabbit.

"This must be pretty boring," said Wing. "I'm telling you all this *about* a poem and I should just make the poem, tell it to you, and stop talking about it. Do you know what I mean?"

"No, not quite," said the rabbit.

"I mean, the things that are *said* about poems are never nearly as interesting as the poems themselves. That's one reason I make poems. Because they're the most interesting way of saying things. In fact, if they're *really* interesting, you won't be able to forget them."

"And what other reasons are there for making poems?" asked the rabbit.

"Maybe there are many other reasons I don't know about, but there is at least one more that I could mention."

"And what's that?"

"It's hard to explain—I'm not sure how to say this— but I make poems because poems help me survive."

"How could that be?"

"Well, let's say you made up a poem about an enemy—Fox for instance. Don't you think that if you could describe Fox really well in a poem, that you would know more about Fox's habits as a hunter, and you'd learn how to avoid him more easily?"

"I suppose so, but I don't want to even think about Fox."

At this point, a little fatigued from perching so long, Wing flexed his wings, then opened them up, making a shadow on the ground that completely covered the rabbit, who shuddered and started for her hole. But Wing settled back on his limb, relaxed his grip, made himself smaller again, and the rabbit relaxed too.

"Now I have a favor to ask of you," said Wing.

"What's that?" said the rabbit.

"Would you help me finish my poem about you?"

"What do you want me to do?"

"I would like you to come out to the middle of The Meadow and just sit there so I can observe you. I need to see you sitting there, very still, with your ears aimed upwind, so I can make some mental notes. Then I'll be able to finish my poem."

"But why can't you make notes right here?"

"I have to see you in a more natural place."

"But this *is* natural—right by my home."

"But it's not quite the same."

"I'd like to do it for you, but I don't feel comfortable leaving my home right now."

"Why not? All I want to do is take some notes so I can celebrate your uniqueness in a poem. I'll even dedicate it to you when I'm finished."

"No thanks," said the rabbit, leaning toward her hole again, her legs tensing.

"Okay," said Wing, "I must be going—thanks anyway. I'll see you later."

"You really mean that, don't you?" said the rabbit.

"Mean what?" said Wing.

"When you say 'See you later,' you mean it in a different way than others—you mean it with your eyes," said the rabbit.

"Yes, that makes sense," said Wing, and he sprung straight up and away.

A half-hour later, flying very high over The Woods, Wing had several thoughts in his head. One of them was that from now on he was just going to shut his beak and mind his own business. Another one was that he'd love to celebrate a certain rabbit's uniqueness with his sharp talons.

4: A Letter from the Possums

Sniff's next task of the morning was to go to The Hole and read Owl's mail. As was his habit, he opened the heavier letters first because they contained coins for autographs. One of the letters was from Grandma Possum:

Dear Owl,

We think you are great. We are so proud to be living in The Woods because we can have you for our leader. We are enclosing one dollar for your autograph. We will pick up the autograph later.

Thank you so much!
The Possum Family

Sniff quickly left The Oak and, carrying a portfolio, hurried over to the Possums' den, where he was met by Grandma Possum. As was often the case, Grandpa Possum was napping and snoring in his favorite corner, and had a smile on his face that seemed to imply that he was dead but at the same time enjoying his nap.

Sniff smiled. "We have just received your wonderful letter," he said.

"We?" asked Grandma Possum.

"Well, you know," said Sniff, "Owl and I have received your wonderful letter, and we want to let you know that your kindness and thoughtfulness are very much appreciated."

"But the letter was for Owl," said Grandma Possum.

"Yes, we understand," said Sniff. "But I am here on behalf of Owl, who asks me to respond in person to such wonderful personal letters like yours."

"I see," she said.

"Now then," he said, "we want you to know that we do very much appreciate such personal greetings, and we do appreciate the money for the autograph. But unfortunately, there is one problem I must inform you of."

"Problem?" she asked.

"Well, yes, please let me explain," he said. "Very simply, the problem is this: the price of autographs has gone up to two dollars."

"Two dollars?" said Grandma Possum.

"Yes. You see, we need two dollars instead of one dollar because Owl is now twice as famous as he was in former times, especially since he's close to retirement. Therefore, since Owl is twice as famous, the price of autographs has doubled."

"I see," said Grandma Possum.

"But let me explain further," said Sniff, sniffing. "Since the price of autographs has gone up to two dollars, we are now—I mean, Owl is now—signing his name two times. Look, I have something for you." He pulled a piece of paper out of his portfolio and held it up so Grandma Possum could read it. "Best Wishes, Owl" was written on the paper two times, the second one directly under the first.

"But why did Owl sign two times if he wasn't sure if we were gonna give another dollar?" asked Grandma Possum. "We don't have very much money."

Sniff smiled. "Well," he said, "we assumed that you would want to pay for two autographs from the greatest leader in the history of The Woods. And you must understand that you are special to us and that I wouldn't have taken the time and effort to come to your place if we didn't think your letter was extra important and heartfelt."

"Thank you for your kindness," Grandma Possum said, her face slightly flushing.

"You're welcome," said Sniff. "And in fact, there is one more reason I am making a personal visit. You see, after the great Owl retires in two weeks, we want to frame a number of special letters, including your letter, and put them on display on The Big Limb. You should feel very special because your letter has been chosen out of hundreds as one of the letters to be framed."

"Oh," she said, "how nice of you to want to frame our letter."

"It is our privilege, of course," said Sniff. "There is just one more problem, however."

"And what is that?" said Grandma Possum.

"Framing the letter will cost the letter writer a dollar," said Sniff. "After all, frames are not cheap, you know."

"Yes, but as I said, we don't have much money," said Grandma Possum. "I'm not sure if—"

"I'll tell you what I'll do," said Sniff, breaking in, looking around and speaking in a hushed tone, sniffing quietly. "Because your letter is so valuable to us, I will pay for the framing personally. All you need to do is give me another dollar for the extra autograph, and I will personally see to it that your great letter is beautifully framed and displayed on The Big Limb after Owl's retirement."

"Oh, I'm so pleased," said Grandma Possum, smiling proudly, flushing again.

"Is it a deal, then?" said Sniff, and gave her the piece of paper.

"It's a deal," Grandma Possum said and rushed away. A moment later she came back with a dollar and gave it to Sniff, smiling.

"This is from the money we were saving for emergencies," she said. "But having our letter framed is more important than that."

"You are right," Sniff said, and took the money graciously. "Thank you. Goodbye."

After he left, Grandma Possum couldn't wait to tell her news to Grandma Squirrel, who lived in a tree nearby.

"I just got the most wonderful news," she said.

"Oh yes? What is it?" asked Grandma Squirrel.

"Sniff came to our place and"—she was so excited she had to stop and start over. "Sniff came to our place and said he is having our letter to Owl framed and displayed on The Big Limb after Owl retires."

"Do you know something?" said Grandma Squirrel, flicking her tail. "This is quite a coincidence because, just last week, Sniff gave me a good deal for having our letter framed too. We must be really good letter writers."

"That's for sure," said Grandma Possum. "And did he say that it would cost an extra dollar for a second autograph?"

"Yes," said Grandma Squirrel, "but Sniff is so generous. He paid for the framing with his own money."

"You know, that's exactly what he did for us too," said Grandma Possum.

"I can't wait to see our letter on display," said Grandma Squirrel.

"Yes, that's for sure," said Grandma Possum. "Won't we be the envy of The Woods?" Then Grandma Possum said goodbye and left.

5: Morning Maneuvers

The Five were lined up in a row, as Sniff began pacing back and forth in front of them, looking over each one, sticking his whiskers into each face in turn, scowling at each pair of eyes, sniffing. He stopped at Number Two:

"Now listen up, Number Two," he said, and sniffed.

"Yeah, sir," said Number Two.

"You got a good pair of gnawing teeth and you got four legs and you got a thin tail. Right?"

"Yeah, sir."

"Now look at Number Three standing beside you."

Number Two turned his eyes and looked at Number Three.

"You see? Number Three's got a good pair of gnawing teeth and four legs and a thin tail—is that right?"

"Yeah, sir."

"So, you're equal. Is that right?"

"Yeah, sir."

"Would you give your life to save Number Three?"

"Ah, yeah sir," said Number Two.

"What?" said Sniff.

"Yeah, sir!" shouted Number Two. Sniff looked up into the trees' high branches.

"Why would you give your life to save Number Three, Number Two?"

"Because, sir, I'm a rat—like him."

"You ain't *like* him, Number Two, you *are* him!"

"Yeah, sir!"

Sniff looked at Number Three.

"And Number Three, look at Number Two standing next to you." Number Three turned his eyes and looked at Number Two.

"Would you give your life to save Number Two?"

"Yeah, sir!"

"Why?"

"Because I'm *him*, sir!"

Sniff took a few steps toward Number One.

"And Number One, would you give your life to save all of the rest of your brothers?"

"Yeah, sir!"

"That's what we're all about," said Sniff, scanning The Five, his look changing to a half-smile, half-sneer. "We are all about togetherness; we are all about sacrifice. And who's our First Enemy? Fox. And he's our *Outside* Enemy. We can't deal with Fox on our own, separately. It can't be done. But we can deal with him if we're united. We are one animal. We are nobody alone. We are no longer individuals. We seek no glory, no rewards. Glory and rewards are for individuals. We are a pack, a colony, a plague, a swarm. All as one, together. All as one. Amen."

Sniff began to walk up and down the line again, his head down, as if studying the ground. "And now, regarding our Second Enemy, our *Inside* Enemy." He paused, looked up. "Number Four, get over here," he said.

Number Four hurried over to Sniff. "Number Four, who is our Second Enemy, our *Inside* Enemy?"

"Old Woods animals, sir!"

"And who are the Old Woods animals?"

"The ones with wings, sir, and the climbers, and the ones without a thin tail, sir!"

"Unless we like 'em," said Sniff.

"Yeah, sir, unless we like 'em, sir!"

"Okay, get back in line." Number Four stepped quickly back in line. Sniff turned his look on Number Five. "Number Five, bite Number Four on the nose as hard as you can."

"Sir, I—"

"Bite him on the nose as hard as you can—NOW!" Number Five bit Number Four on the nose as hard as he could and Number Four squeaked and staggered backward a few steps, then got back in line, and stood at attention.

"Did you feel that, Number Four?" asked Sniff, suddenly looking at Number Four.

"Ah, no sir!" said Number Four.

"Do it again, Number Five," said Sniff. "Bite him *hard*." Number Five bit Number Four on the nose again and Number Four squeaked, staggered, and righted himself.

"Did you feel that one, Number Four?" said Sniff.

"Yeah, sir!" said Number Four.

"Where did you feel it, Number Four?"

"On my nose, sir!" said Number Four.

"How about right *here*," said Sniff, sticking a paw in the center of Number Four's chest, poking him three times.

"In the chest, sir!" said Number Four.

"Where?"

"In the heart, sir!"

"Okay. Number Four. Bite Number Two on a leg as hard as you can." Number Four took a few steps and bit Number Two on a leg and Number Two squeaked.

"Hard!" shouted Sniff. Number Four bit Number Two's leg again and he squeaked again, staggered backward, then got back in line.

"Did you feel that, Number Four?" said Sniff.

"Yeah, sir!"

"Where?"

"In my heart, sir!"

"Where?"

"In my heart, sir!"

"Did you all feel it equally?" said Sniff, scanning the others, searching their eyes, sniffing.

"Yeahhhhhhhhhh, sir!" shouted The Five in unison.

"Now look here, Number Five," said Sniff, pointing at him. "Is Number Two the Enemy?"

"No, sir!"

"Has he got wings?"

"No, sir!"

"Is he a bird brain?"

"No, sir!"

"Does he climb trees or live in the branches of a tree?"

"No, sir!"

"Does he have a bushy tail?"

"No, sir!"

"Does he write po-etry?"

"No, sir!"

"Then why did you bite him, Number Four?" asked Sniff.

"Because you told me to, sir!" said Number Four.

"Do you do everything I tell you to do?"

"Yeah, sir!"

"You got it," said Sniff, smiling. Then he continued, and turned to Number Two. "Now, tell us who our friends are, Number Two."

"New Woods animals, sir!" said Number Two.

"And who are the New Woods animals?" asked Sniff, now looking at Number One.

"The animals that hate Old Woods animals, sir!" said Number One.

"You got it," said Sniff. He paced again, up and down the line. "And what do we intend to do about the Enemy, Number Three?"

"Eliminate it, sir!" said Number Three. His voice was masculine, certain.

"You got it," said Sniff. "'Eliminate.' Good word. All of you, say it as one, say it together. E-LIM-I-NATE."

"E-LIM-I-NATE," said The Five, in one voice. Then Sniff walked up to Number One and whispered softly into his ear: "Today's quota—six." Then Number One turned to Number Two and whispered softly into his ear: "Today's quota—six." And so on down the line the message went, until Number Five got it from Number Four.

"Amen," said Sniff rather quietly.

"Amen, sir," said The Five together, softly, in one voice, as one animal with five thin tails, twenty legs, and five sets of gnawing teeth, shining in the morning sunlight.

6: A Difference of Opinion

Wing and Butterfly were in the habit of getting together and exchanging ideas. On this day, perched on one of their favorite branches in an ash tree, the conversation began, as it often did, with a question from Wing.

"Let me ask you, my friend, which is easier and more important to remember—being hurt or being helped by another animal?"

"I would say being helped," said Butterfly.

"I don't agree," said Wing.

"Why not?" said Butterfly.

"Okay," said Wing, "let's say that after a fight with another hawk, I had a torn wing. I wouldn't forget that injury—which could put my life in danger by hindering my flying—and neither could I forget the hawk that inflicted the injury since, every time I saw him, I'd fear for my life. Now, let's say that same hawk, sometime later, for some unknown reason helped me escape from Fox, who suddenly ambushed me when I was feeding on a fresh kill in The Meadow. Now tell me—which would I remember best: the hawk's hurting me or his helping me?"

"You would remember being helped because you could then help him someday when he was in trouble," said Butterfly.

"I think you're wrong," said Wing, "although I do of course realize that being helped by another animal is also important and useful not only to the one helped but also the helper. And by the way, it seems like the longer I live, the more I notice that whenever I shift my attention to one or the other side of an argument or conflict, if I look closely, both sides can become equally convincing to me."

"But tell me," said Butterfly, "why would you remember being hurt better than being helped?"

"It's just that we tend to learn more from bad experiences than from good ones," said Wing, "because the memories of the bad experiences are more apt to keep us alive. It's good to have those bad experiences in our memory, so we're able to avoid them in the future. And after all, my survival is far more important to me than any other hawk's survival."

"Yes," said Butterfly. "But don't you think that kind of reasoning, if carried too far, can make an animal selfish?"

"Selfish?" said Wing. "All of us are selfish."

"But isn't it also true that all of us have an unselfish side?" said Butterfly.

"Yes," said Wing. "We're both unselfish and selfish at the same time. But the selfishness comes more naturally, day to day, minute to minute, than the unselfishness. Those who are oblivious to their in-born selfishness, or worse yet, who go around pretending as if they're altogether unselfish, can be very dangerous animals."

"But to assume," said Butterfly, "that we are by nature more selfish than unselfish can be dangerous too, since it can provide a ready-made excuse for being selfish. It's like assuming that we might as well be mean, instead of kind, since everybody else is more mean than kind. So, we're forced to keep on assuming that others are always trying to take advantage of us."

"Or," said Wing, "knowing that we're more selfish than unselfish by nature can provide a reason to be *aware* of our selfishness, whenever possible. And isn't it interesting how an act of benevolence can be at the same time selfish, since it can bring much praise from others, and consequently raise one's status in The Woods, and even the amount on one's paycheck?"

"Does that then make the act any less benevolent?" asked Butterfly.

"Not at all," said Wing. "It's still benevolence. I'm just saying that our actions are not simply one-sided."

"Maybe what we're talking about today," said Butterfly, "applies especially to at least one animal among us."

"Yes," said Wing, "The one animal who is no doubt responsible for more and more lifeless bodies of non-rats scattered around. Do you agree?"

"I agree," said Butterfly. "All those uneaten carcasses can't be just from Fox, can they? Fox doesn't kill just to be killing."

"That's right," said Wing. "You and I know that Sniff and The Five are responsible for the demise of a whole lot of them. And what's even scarier is that this animal with a thin tail and gnawing teeth and four legs, who calls himself a leader—and those who are different, followers—intends to become the one and only leader of us all, after Owl retires in a couple of weeks."

"I think you are right," said Butterfly.

"Let's keep this rat in mind," said Wing, "and maybe the two of us can eventually come up with a way to deal with him."

"Yes," said Butterfly, "let's keep talking."

Then the two good friends said goodbye and flew away in opposite directions.

7: Dream of the Week

The winning dream on this Saturday morning was Stub's. Every morning before maneuvers, The Five—co-rats of The Dream Committee—conducted a dream survey, after which Number One would report especially interesting dreams to Sniff, head rat of the committee. Then on Saturday morning, after receiving the list of the three dreams judged best, Sniff would choose The Dream of the Week. The winner was awarded a certificate, and two dollars.

Stub's dream was about dark, subterranean passages—some long and winding, some short and sharp-turning. About dead ends. About walls. About animals getting lost in the dark, unable to find their way out. About getting caught and eaten.

"Hey, thank you," said Stub, when Sniff presented him his certificate.

"How many does that make now? Four winning dreams?" said Sniff.

"Nine," said Stub, realizing that Sniff wasn't holding any money. "And my prize money will be coming later?"

"Well," said Sniff, sniffing, "this week you and I had to split the award, since we both had equally unusual and wonderful dreams. So you get the certificate and I get the money."

"Really?" said Stub. "And what was your dream about?"

"My dream was about dark passages," said Sniff, "and dead ends, and animals getting lost."

"That's interesting," said Stub. "It sounds just like the dream I had, about a maze."

"Yes, a maze," said Sniff. "We all thought it was quite a coincidence. But your dream was of course an underground dream. The committee felt that my dream was more appropriate because most of us animals, especially the leaders, live above ground."

"I see," said Stub. "Most of my dreams are about being underground, so maybe they're not so appropriate."

"Anyway," said Sniff, "we certainly had a wonderful dream, didn't we?"

"I guess so," said Stub, and the two went on their way.

8: A Collaboration

Immediately after the conversation with Stub, Sniff went to Spider. She was hanging upside down in her web, resting, and waiting for the *twang* of a snagged bug. Sniff reached up and tweaked the web a couple of times. Startled by the vibration, Spider automatically moved toward it, and when she was close enough to see Sniff, she said, "What're you doing that for?"

Sniff sniffed. "I've got an idea about a building project, and I wonder if you'd be interested."

"What sort of a project are you talking about?" said Spider, looking at Sniff with her six little eyes.

"I'd like to have a maze built for public recreation," he said. "What do you think? Would you be interested in designing it?"

"You mean one of those things that have a lot of sharp turns and dead-ends—that you have to find your way through and out of?" said Spider.

"That's right," said Sniff. "Stub could be your chief consultant, since he knows a lot about secret passages, and The Five, with help from others, could do the work. All you'd have to do is design it."

"But I've never designed anything like a maze before," Spider said.

"I understand," said Sniff, "but I'm talking about a community project, an ideal way to carry on The Great Tradition. You are a wonderful architect, the best in The Woods. What a great contribution you'd be making to the community."

"You mean you want me to do the designing for free?" asked Spider.

"Well, yes, this would be a donation to The Woods by its most superb architect," said Sniff.

"I don't work for free. Maybe somebody else would like to help you," Spider said, and began turning away.

"Wait—I've got an even better idea," said Sniff.

"What's that?" said Spider, who stopped, turned, and faced Sniff again, her little eyes glimmering.

"Let's say you could kill two birds with one acorn with this project," said Sniff. "First, you could make a great contribution to the community, and second, you could spin some webs inside the maze and catch more bugs."

"That wouldn't be too practical," said Spider. "If I committed myself to building a maze, I wouldn't want to be doing two things at once. A maze is a maze, a web is a web."

"So," Sniff said, "you're not interested in making a contribution to the community. Is that right?"

"I didn't say that, *you* said that," said Spider, looking a little perturbed.

"Well, that's what it sounds like to me," said Sniff, and he turned around and started walking away.

"Wait a minute," said Spider. "Come back here."

"What for?" asked Sniff, turning around.

"Could you maybe call this a donation, let me have some webs, and also pay me a little on the side?" said Spider.

"How much?" asked Sniff.

"How many webs are you talking about?" asked Spider.

"I would think five would be a good number," said Sniff.

"How about six?" said Spider.

"That would work," said Sniff.

"And how much of a fee are we talking about then?" asked Spider.

"How about five dollars?" said Sniff.

"Make it six?" said Spider.

"I suppose I could come up with six," said Sniff.

"When do we start?" asked Spider.

"How about if I send Stub over to you and you two could get started on the design today?" said Sniff. "I'd like to get going on the maze as soon as possible."

"That's fine," said Spider.

And so that's how a collaboration, like a brand-new spider web, glittering in the sunlight, was launched.

9: The Maze

Spider was excited about the prospect of spinning more webs for more food and was able—with some help from Stub—to produce a blueprint in just a couple of hours. Construction began that same afternoon and would continue overnight into Sunday morning. The Maze was built close to The Oak, but still with enough room between the outer walls and The Big Limb to accommodate a crowd, during an Appearance, or other events. Stub and six other moles dug grooves in the ground; meanwhile, The Five, along with four other rats, pounded pieces of bark upright in the grooves. The pieces of bark—rough side out—were lined up so close together that a mouse's whisker could not be wedged between them. Planks were pounded into the ground to support the walls.

The Maze was fairly dim inside, because of its close proximity to The Oak and several other overhanging trees with heavy fall leaf cover, and because its walls were slanted slightly inward. The passages were wide enough to accommodate animals as large as minks, but not wide enough for porcupines or beavers (Sniff had said during the construction, "After all, everything has its limits").

The maze-route required many left and right turns. There were ten dead-ends, and Spider, according to the agreement with Sniff, had happily spun her webs in six of them. Some animals had watched the construction, standing on the safe side of a sign that said: "Keep Out—Animals at Work." Sniff was present the entire time, moving busily inside the walls, feeling and sniffing them as they were being assembled.

After a final inspection by Spider and Sniff, The Maze was pronounced so solid that no flood or hail could damage it, no ice could crack it.

Just outside the entrance to The Maze, a sign saying, "The Beginning," printed in bold red letters on a piece of bark, was stuck in the ground; on the opposite side, where an animal emerged after its run-through, was a second sign saying, "The End."

Standing on The Big Limb, Number Two said in his resonant voice several times that Sniff would be making an important announcement from The Oak the next day, "Opening Day, at six p.m." Then he added, "All those who show up will receive a special, free gift."

10: Learning the Way

Shortly after noon on Sunday, Sniff, The Five, and Spider met at the Beginning. Spider was carrying her blueprint, with the maze-route—newly designated by Sniff as *The Way*—highlighted in red ink.

"Listen up, rats," said Sniff as he sniffed and pointed with a flourish at The Maze. "What we have in front of us here represents a great challenge. It'll take all of your mental and physical abilities in order to avoid getting confused or lost. Only those animals with a good mind and a good body will succeed. But it's not just figuring out The Way that matters. You will figure it out very soon. What matters most is your speed-of-foot. You will need to be able to move through The Way at top speed. The fastest runners—in other words, the best athletes—will end up as the true winners, the true leaders."

Sniff paused, and looked at The Beginning. "You see, rats," he went on, "The Maze is not recreation. Recreation, don't forget, is for bird-brains." Moving closer to The Five, he stuck his face in the face of Number One, who was slightly larger than the others:

"You hear?" Sniff said, quietly, personally.

"Yeah, sir," said Number One, looking at the entrance.

"The pressure is on you," said Sniff. "What you do the others will do. You mess up, they mess up; you do a good job, they do a good job. You hear?"

"Yeah, sir," said Number One, rigid, staring seriously.

"Okay, listen up," said Sniff, stepping away. "I want all of you to line up behind me and Spider, and as we go through, I want you to sniff and feel around, keep your eyes wide open, and memorize The Way of The Maze. Study it. Learn it. Lock it into your nose, your brain, your legs, and feet. You got it?"

"Yeah, sir!" shouted The Five together, all twenty legs tensing for action.

Sniff began to move with caution just behind Spider, who squinted down at her blueprint as she moved forward. Just as Sniff said "Go," he punched the timer on his stopwatch, took his first step, stumbled and nearly fell, then righted himself. The Five followed closely behind. All the while, as they advanced, now stumbling at times in their new and strange environment, now moving straight ahead, now turning left, then right, two steps one way, three another, at times halting, and looking around, puzzled, turning this way and that, sniffing, their whiskers twitching, their noses taking it all in . . . as Spider, leading the way, kept checking and following the red line of her elaborate blueprint, and Sniff kept talking: "This way," he said. "No, this way—here—not that way. This way— wait—now where? This way—sniff around, feel the walls, memorize, study. Memorize The Way. Discover The Way of the Maze, The Way of Life. Learn it now and forever. Never forget it. This way. Not that way—*here*—this way. Smell the bark, feel it. Feel the walls—see them. This way—*here*. Now *here—smell here, here, right here*," he said, pointing to the walls and touching them as he talked.

When they came to The End and Spider and Sniff, breathing hard, stepped out, Sniff clicked the timer on his watch. "Eight minutes and eighteen seconds," he said. Then he looked back and admonished The Five—just as the last feet were emerging, like the backend of a centipedal rat. "See this daylight?" he pointed at the clear sky, "this is what you move toward, this is your goal, always. Don't forget it—it's just like life itself—you're always beginning in the dark and moving toward the light. In life there's always plenty of sharp turns, blind alleys, and dead ends; you're always bumping into or about to bump into barriers and walls, always up against the unpredictable, but you eventually smell victory and then come out victorious. In life, you go from the beginning to the end, which is what is also known as going from darkness to light. Isn't that what so many of the po-ets say in their po-ems? Haha."

"Yeahhhhh, sir!" shouted The Five in unison, once more standing in a rigid row, somewhat less alert-looking than when they went in. All of them were blinking in the sunlight. Several were picking strands of spider webs off their legs. All of them, Sniff noticed—except Number Three—were breathing hard, but not as loud as Sniff himself, and Spider, who was still checking her blueprint.

"Number Three, get over here," Sniff said, and Number Three complied. "How come you're not breathing very hard, like the rest of us?"

"I don't know, sir," said Number Three, "I guess it's because I'm not tired."

"You went through this maze like the others, didn't you?" said Sniff.

"Yeah, sir," said Number Three, "but it was pretty easy for me."

"That's amazing," said Sniff. "But here's another question for you. What else are you moving toward, inside that maze, besides the light?"

"Sir?" said Number Three.

"What is the main thing, Number Three," said Sniff, still breathing audibly, "that you want to eliminate from The Woods?" Sniff smelled Number Three's face, then picked up a squirrel's tail, which he had dropped on the ground earlier just outside The End, held it up in front of Number Three's beady eyes, and shook it several times.

"Squirrels?" said Number Three.

"Yes, true, but this is a symbol—a symbol of Fox," said Sniff, shaking the tail again. "You got it half right, at least. Not just Fox and squirrels but any and all other Old Woods animals—remember?"

"I guess so," said Number Three.

"You guess so," said Sniff, who then backed away from Number Three and began to address all of The Five again. He picked up a stick, which, earlier, he had gnawed to a sharp end, took a piece of cord lying nearby, tied the tail to the stick and thrust it into a ready-made hole in the ground, and pounded on it a few times, so that the squirrel tail would be the first thing noticed by an animal emerging from The End.

"Here it is," Sniff went on. "Here is something we don't just *guess* we hate—we hate it so much we want to eliminate it from The Woods. Right?"

"Riiiiiiight, sir!" all five yelled together.

"Then get over here and smell it," said Sniff, "get all over it with your noses. Now!" All of them rushed over to the tail and got all over it with their noses, sniffing, sniffing.

"You got it," Sniff said. "You run to the light, and you run to *this*." He held the squirrel tail straight out on the stick and pointed to it. "Light—and the Enemies. All of the enemies in The Woods."

Sniff stepped away from the tail. "Okay, once more," he said, "get around there and do it again (pointing to the wall of The Maze)—line up, and when you hear me yell *Go*! I want you to get through this maze in under six minutes, and I mean it. And this time, get all those turns, left and right, into your clever little rat brains."

The Five scurried quickly around the walls and lined up at The Beginning, in single file. When he knew they'd had time to get ready, Sniff yelled "Go!" just as he punched his timer, and they plunged inside.

Sniff was looking at his watch and counting just as The Five exploded out, screaming *"Enemy, Enemy, Enemy!"* all of them breathing audibly, except Number Three. "Seven minutes, thirty-one seconds—too slow, you groundlings. Get back there and do it again." They all ran around to the front and plunged through The Beginning again at Sniff's command, and again came out into daylight, and (except for Number Three) panting. All were cursing the squirrel tail, close to where Sniff was standing.

"Seven minutes, fourteen—too slow, you dirty rats, way too slow. You hear?"

"Yeahhhhh, sir!" they yelled, all but Number Three working to catch their breath, and sweating.

"Listen up," said Sniff, "This time you get back there and I mean MOVE!"

"Yeahhhhhhhhhh, sir!" they shouted together.

"What did you say?" said Sniff.

"Yeahhhhhhhhhhhhhhhhh, sir!" The shout was piercing, teeth showing.

"And I don't wanna hear any hard breathing when you come out this time. Right?"

"Riiiiiiiight sir!"

This time The Five finished in three ticks under seven minutes.

"Terrible, awful, but better," said Sniff. All of them (except, once again, Number Three) were trying to hold their hard breathing in check, as they stood there, tense-whiskered, staring at nothing. Most of them had strands of webs on their legs.

"Now hear me, rats," said Sniff. "From now on, every day, first thing in the morning I want you over here running this maze. The main thing is to lock The Way into your life, to show, by example, that you're the leaders, you're the best and fastest athletes in The Woods. That means I don't want you through there in anything over five minutes and thirty seconds. You hear?"

"Yeahhhhhhhhhh, sir!" The Five stared straight ahead—obedient.

"That's more like it," said Sniff, and he turned and walked away, clutching the blueprint, with Spider beside him, her eight little legs racing to keep up.

11: Opening Day

It was Monday at six p.m. Sniff was standing above the crowd on The Big Limb, holding a microphone. Next to him was Number Two, holding a piece of paper. Wing and Butterfly were settled on a limb fairly close to The Big Limb, and Claws was on another limb, close by. Sniff thanked Spider, The Five, and Stub for their work on The Maze. Then he said (gesturing toward The Maze): "Animals of The Woods, as you can see, I came through on my promise to carry on The Great Tradition, and I can say, without hesitation, that learning The Way of the Maze, and then continuous practice, and faster and faster times, will be the best possible preparation for fighting and defeating Fox. Not to mention the fact that the fastest maze-runners will be the best possible candidates for leader of The Woods, when Owl retires, which will be soon." There was some applause, and after it died down, Wing yelled out, "All for you rats—Yeah, yeah, yeah!" Then he flew to a branch much closer to Sniff, and when he landed, looked at Sniff and then down at the crowd: "Everybody knows that rats are better at running mazes than other animals. This maze is all for the rats!"

Sniff ignored Wing, sniffed, and went on: "And now, Number Two will present to you the rules of our magnificent new maze. As you can see, the rules are printed prominently on the sign standing next to The Maze. Take a look." All heads turned toward the sign, with its conspicuously large red letters.

Sniff gave the microphone to Number Two. "Okay, listen up," he said. "These are The Seven Rules of The Maze," speaking in his loud, articulate way:

"Rule Number One. 'Leaders Will Have First Priority Over Followers'

Rule Number Two: 'Only Running or Walking Allowed—No Climbing the Walls or Flying over the Walls'

Rule Number Three: 'No Cheating, Period'

Rule Number Four: 'All Insects, Free Admittance'

Rule Number Five: 'No Snakes Allowed'

Rule Number Six: 'Cost—Twenty-Five Cents, or Forty Cents for Two Runs'

Rule Number Seven: 'Absolutely No Refunds!'"

When Number Two finished, there was some chattering in the crowd. Some were concerned about the cost, others were puzzled by the "no refunds" rule, and the "first priority" rule. Two doves were conversing about the second rule: "So if we can't fly?" said one of them, "we'll have to run or walk, like the rats and others—is that how you understand it?"

"That's how I see it," said the other dove, "and I don't think it's fair."

"I don't think so, either," said the first dove. "And what about frogs—they're hoppers and they can hop through The Maze, but we're fliers, and we can't fly through it? Is hopping the same as walking or running?"

"I don't think so," said the other dove.

Once again, Wing spoke up, addressing the crowd: "Who doesn't know—anybody here today—that rats are genetically inclined to be good maze runners!"

Sniff grabbed the microphone from Number Two. "Genetically inclined?" he said, "that's pretty fancy phrasing, even for a po-et. But listen: maybe you birds would be good at running a maze, you're graceful up in the air, aren't you? You'll never know until you try it. But don't forget—the rule says 'no flying over the walls." Sniff laughed, and many in the crowd laughed too.

Then came the grand finale. Sniff quieted the crowd. He looked over to The Hole, and after several seconds, taking his time again, Owl stepped out, gripping a large sign made of bark, took his three famous steps, then walked off into the air, swooped grandly down and over the crowd, landed, placed the sign on a tripod near The Beginning, and flew away into the trees, as the crowd cheered loudly.

Number Two quickly descended to the ground, walked over to the sign, now prominently displayed, and read it aloud, and loud:

THE SNIFF MAZE
CONCEIVED AND DESIGNED BY
OWL AND SNIFF

There was a sudden burst of applause all around Number Two, causing him to smile. Both Stub and Spider looked at each other, agreeing with their looks that their names also could've been displayed on the sign, for all of their hard work, and of course, the fact that The Maze came out of Stub's original dream, and was designed by Spider.

"That word Number Two read, 'conceived.' What does that mean?" said one mink to another.

"I think it means something like 'dreamed up,'" said the second mink.

"Oh," said the first mink, "Sniff must be quite a dreamer."

Two squirrels talking to each other agreed that the "no climbing the walls" phrase was too harsh.

Standing on The Big Limb, Sniff had one more announcement: "Listen up, everybody: Your first maze-run is on me—it's my free gift to you all!" Then he waved to the cheering crowd and stepped back inside The Hole. There was great excitement among the animals, and some pushing and shoving as they were getting in line outside The Beginning, eager to take their first try at running The Maze.

12: One Mad Squirrel

Most of the animals enjoyed their first try at a maze-run, especially since it was free, and even though most of them got lost and had to be retrieved by one of The Five, who had been assigned as guides. The only animal who refused help when he got lost was Claws; yet finally, after several frustrating minutes, he too had to be retrieved (by Number Five) and escorted to The End.

When the two emerged, the first thing Claws saw, of course, was the squirrel tail hanging from a stick.

"What's this?" he asked Number Five.

"The Enemy," said Number Five.

"The Enemy?" Claws said. "A squirrel tail?"

"That's a fox tail, the Enemy," said Number Five.

"You're crazy if you don't know the difference between a fox tail and a squirrel tail," said Claws. "Look." He held up his bushy tail to Number Five, then huffed away and went directly over to the Oak to find Sniff, who was resting among the roots.

"I don't care much for your maze," said Claws.

"What's the problem?" said Sniff

"It's way too complicated," said Claws.

"Oh," said Sniff, "it sounds like you had a little trouble figuring out The Way?"

"Maybe I did, like everybody else," said Claws, his eyes seriously wide open.

"And maybe you're not the athletic type?" said Sniff.

"I've never been known to be slow or awkward on my feet, I can tell you that," said Claws.

"Well then," said Sniff, "if it's not a physical problem, it's something else. Maybe you've heard of the story about the jackrabbit and the crab apple?"

"No, I haven't," said Claws.

"Once there was a jackrabbit who tried to grab a crab apple hanging from a high branch," said Sniff. "But it was too high, and he couldn't quite reach it."

"And so?" said Claws.

"He tried to knock the crab apple out of the tree with a few walnuts," said Sniff, "but that didn't work either, so he turned around and went home. After all, when you realize you can't accomplish a particular goal in life, why not just give up and go home?"

"You ever see me give up?" said Claws.

"Not yet," said Sniff. "Just don't forget the rule about climbing the walls."

"I don't break rules, either," said Claws. "But here's another question for you."

"What's that?" asked Sniff.

"What's the business with the squirrel tail?" said Claws.

"Oh yes," said Sniff. "The squirrel tail was put there for military maneuvers. It's a symbol—a symbol of Fox."

"It's an insult to squirrels," said Claws.

"It's too bad we couldn't use a *real* fox tail," said Sniff. "The Five were on patrol a while back and found a dead squirrel, so we used its tail instead. You do know what a symbol is, don't you?"

"So now you're insulting me again?" said Claws, and before Sniff could respond he abruptly leaped high over him, making him flinch, stuck to The Oak like a four-pronged dart, hesitated a moment, then climbed quickly and gracefully straight up, glancing back down at his detractor who (he was happy to witness) was getting smaller and smaller just as he, a nimble squirrel, was rising higher and higher.

13: Grandpa Possum Tells a Story

It was a sound like no other sound in The Woods. It was a familiar sound, like the two clean notes of a chickadee, or a frog's mournful croaking. But this sound was different because the two synchronized notes—which always occurred in tandem—usually came from different parts of The Woods.

Never did one sound occur by itself, no matter how far the sounds were separated from each other. If the sound began with a *WE*, it ended with an *I*. If it began with an *I*, it ended with a *WE*. The intensity and loudness of the first sound was matched exactly by the intensity and loudness of the second one. Each sound was both at war and in harmony with the other sound.

One night, the Possums' two grandsons were visiting them. Hearing the sound, the older grandson asked his grandpa: "What's that sound?"

"Ah, yes. There's a story behind it," said his grandpa, who was usually dozing or asleep, but when awake, liked to tell stories to his grandsons. "Would you like me to tell it to you?"

"Me too," said the younger grandson. "Tell us."

"Once upon a time," said Grandpa Possum, "there was a hawk and a rat. Each one had his own belief about life in The Woods. The rat believed in the way of the pack. For him, individual animals didn't count, only the pack, the group, counted. But the hawk was different. For him, only the individual was important.

"Now it is not unusual for two animals to have different beliefs. But these two animals were very stubborn about their beliefs, which were as natural to them as breathing itself.

"And so, they could never get along. In fact, they were so different in their beliefs that every word, every smile or bad look, every gesture, every thought, every hope or dream of one of them was a horrible insult to the other.

"Over the years, they came to an agreement: to despise each other in all ways."

"Despise?" said the younger grandson.

"It means hate," said Grandpa Possum. "They hated each other.

"Now sometimes it happens," Grandpa Possum went on, "that since the two animals lived in the same woods, if they saw each other too often, their hatred might become harmful, or even deadly. Because of this, they avoided each other whenever possible. And that was another strong agreement between the rat and the hawk: to avoid each other as much as possible.

"One day, looking for food, the rat and the hawk happened to meet in the middle of The Woods. They looked at each other, and their eyes froze and burned at the same time, just as the rat's claws and the hawk's talons became extremely tense. Suddenly the hawk said, *'I'* and then the rat said, *'We.'* Then the rat said, *'We,'* and the hawk said, *'I.'* The words, as they faced each other, became louder and louder and longer and longer: *IIIIIII …WEEEEEEE.* At that moment, they both agreed that the length and intensity of the shouting should always be equal. After several minutes of shouting at each other, they stopped; then the rat scrambled away and the hawk flew away."

"Did you say 'talons'? What are they?" asked the younger grandson.

"They are the claws of the hawk," said Grandpa Possum, who went on: "From that day on, the sound of the hawk and the rat shouting at each other in the middle of The Woods became known as the *I-WE*. And so, whenever you hear that sound, it's the sound of the hawk and the rat, disagreeing and agreeing at the same time."

Grandpa Possum paused, waiting for a response from his grandsons.

"And what about the rat and the hawk?" asked the younger grandson. "Do they still hate each other?"

"Yes, they do," said Grandpa Possum.

"What if you heard only the *I* or only the *WE*?" said the older grandson.

"I suppose," said Grandpa Possum, "that would mean that one or the other is dead or gone very far away."

"But why would one of them go on making his own sound when the other is gone or dead?" asked the younger grandson.

"I don't know," said Grandpa Possum. "I suppose it could mean that one of them had won the war between them, or maybe that the one that's still around feels bad that the other one is gone or dead. Or maybe he feels both bad and good at the same time."

"But I wonder why he would need to go on making his sound if the other one was not around to hear him?" asked the older grandson.

"Well," said Grandpa Possum, "it could mean that they agreed in the beginning that their hatred for each other was forever. And maybe that's the final agreement between them: to go on and on hating each other forever. And so, when one is dead or gone from The Woods, the other must go on with his *I* or his *We*. Maybe, come to think of it, it's a way of showing some respect for all the things that they agreed on together." Grandpa Possum smiled.

"But if they hate each other so much, why do they agree on so many things?" asked the older grandson.

"That *is* unusual, I'll admit," said Grandpa Possum. "Now tell me, what is the main thing the story is about, do you think?" He looked at one and then at the other.

"Well," said the older grandson, "it means that if the rat and the hawk can agree to hate each other, and on so many other things, maybe they could agree to get along better."

"That is a good idea," said Grandpa Possum.

"To me, the story is about hate," said the younger grandson. "All it makes me think about is hate."

"But what does the story make you want to *do*, if anything?" asked Grandpa Possum. Again, he looked at one, and then the other.

"Nothing, right now, because I don't hate anybody," said the younger grandson. "But if I hated somebody and I heard the story, and the sound, it would make me hate more."

"But doesn't the story make you want to choose between the *I* and the *We*?" asked Grandpa Possum.

"Not me," said the younger grandson. "It only makes me think of hate."

"Not me, either," said the older grandson. "It makes me think that it's strange that the rat and the hawk can't get along better if they can agree on so many things."

"Well," said Grandpa Possum, "anyway, it's a story that makes you think, isn't that right?"

"I guess so," said the older grandson, and the younger one said, "I think it's kinda dumb."

After the two youngsters left and went outside to play, Grandpa Possum scratched his head and thought about the story. He was puzzled. Did he tell the story right? Did he forget something, maybe an important detail or two? Maybe he wasn't as good a storyteller as he thought he was? And then, getting drowsier and drowsier, as he began to re-tell the story to himself, he fell asleep.

14: Number Three's Secrets

The Maze would quickly become popular, especially among the four-legged animals, most notably the rats. Very few animals would turn out to be good maze runners—for instance, the rabbits, because they were too jittery, as if escaping a predator, the squirrels, because they were always trying to climb the walls, and the moles and voles, who were simply too ploddingly slow.

On Opening Day Sniff had designated Stub to be the "Volunteer Manager," whose main job was to collect fees, and post record maze-times. Though he disliked having to take on another job and not get paid for it, and was still upset because Sniff hadn't acknowledged him as being a contributor to the origin of The Maze (not to mention the fact that Owl had had nothing to do with it). And yet Stub liked the word "manager" attached to his name, believing that it could have a positive effect on his reputation.

Sniff had designated several rats for other jobs as well: one would serve as the timer, with a stopwatch, stationed in a nearby elm, in a unique spot from which he could see runners enter The Maze, and also exit at The End (though because of the leaf cover, he couldn't see them running *through* The Maze). Two other rats, called vigilantes, were to work inside, one a few steps from The Beginning, and the other a few steps from The End. They had two responsibilities: to make sure that no animals climbed or flew over the walls; and, if any runner who wasn't a rat was moving too fast on any given run, to slow it down by sticking out a leg and tripping it up.

Any rule violations were reported immediately to Stub, who then reported them to Sniff. Cheaters were fined twenty-five cents, and banned from The Maze for two days. Animals that showed up just to watch the runners were charged a "spectator fee" of five cents.

The new maze, which, according to Sniff, was a way of carrying on The Great Tradition, would also turn out to be a money-maker. Most of the fees collected would go to the funds of The Anti-Fox League and The Charity Committee, both of which were headed by Sniff.

It was early in the morning, just after The Five had finished their morning maze run, and were lined up just outside The End.

"Number Three, get over here!" The abrupt, sharp voice was that of Number One. Number Three—at certain junctures and turns that he knew so well already—had unintentionally moved too fast, bumping into Number Two several times, disrupting the pace of The Five.

"You do realize, don't you," said Number One, "that you've been messing up our training sessions?" Number One's beady eyes were a fraction of an inch from the softer eyes of Number Three, who responded by saying, "But I want to improve my time. And I want all of us to be able to run faster times—"

"Now you listen to me," said Number One, his whiskers pressing against Number Three's nose, his voice turning rock-hard: "We are supposed to run this maze as a unit. We are one animal, one-pack. One-body-with-twenty-legs, five-heads, and five-tails. One-big-animal. Only as a unit can we defeat our enemies. This is an exercise in one-ness, all-togetherness. Do you understand?"

"Yeah, sir," said Number Three.

"Then from now on," said Number One, "pack-speed only. You got it?"

"Yeah, sir," said Number Three, and Number One turned away and walked off, looking stiffly arrogant.

Number Three had a few secrets. One of them was his desire to be a great maze runner. Nothing—not Number One's harsh commands, not even Sniff, he was certain—could stifle his desire. Later that day, when he was supposed to be hunting, Number Three left The Five, saying he didn't feel good (he was actually depressed), circled back to The Maze and did three runs. By the end of his second run he was excited, not only because his depression had lifted but because he'd been able to quickly chart out the tricky moves of The Way in his head, and to mutter, under his breath, his steps from The Beginning to The End, starting with *two steps left, one step right, four steps ahead . . . .*

He had also discovered, by the end of his third and final run, that when he repeated the sequence of turns and steps aloud or under his breath as he was running, The Way was more challenging than when he simply ran without thinking about running.

He began to wonder about all this—to think not only about his thinking, but about his not-thinking. On his way home from The Maze, hearing the frogs' deep croaking in The Pond, he decided that if he could talk to Frog, he might be able to learn something that would help him improve his maze-running time.

Frog was there alright—on break—near the bank in the shallow, moss-covered water, waiting for insects to pass over close enough to be snatched out of the air. "Hey Frog!" Number Three called out, sitting on the bank close by, "I've got a question for you." Frog's body automatically shifted in the direction of the question, and he faced his questioner.

"What's your question?" asked Frog.

"Do you ever think about thinking?" asked Number Three.

"Yes/no," said Frog.

"What do you mean, 'yes/no'?" said Number Three.

"I do and I don't," said Frog.

"Would you please explain what you mean?" said Number Three.

"Well, right now," said Frog, "as I'm speaking to you, I'm thinking about thinking, otherwise I wouldn't know what to say to you. And yet, mostly, I don't think too much, let alone think about thinking. I just do what I do."

"Well, then," said Number Three, "what do you think about thinking about thinking? I mean, when you *do* think about it?"

"I think it can be pretty useless," said Frog.

"Oh, really?" said Number Three. "In my case, I've memorized The Way of The Maze, and I can run through it very fast. I can run through pretty much with my eyes closed, or at night when I can't see anything, just giving myself the detailed instructions as I go, all the steps and turns, one by one by one. And yet, I can also run through The Maze without anything in my head to think about. And when I run without anything in my head, I run just as fast, if not faster. It's a strange feeling. Do you know what I mean?"

"Yes/no," said Frog. A fly buzzed over his bulging eyes and he snapped at it but missed.

"But tell me why you think that thinking can be, as you say, 'pretty useless,'" said Number Three. "Don't you think about catching bugs when you're catching them?"

"Yes/no," said Frog.

"But you've memorized how to do it, haven't you?" said Number Three, "and you do teach young frogs how to catch bugs, don't you?"

"Here's what I mean," said Frog. "I know how to catch bugs and I can think of how it's done, and I can teach it with precise details to other frogs, and I do, because that's my job. But it doesn't make any difference, because when I'm hungry, which is most of the time, I just catch bugs and eat them."

"Why don't you demonstrate what it's like to catch a bug by thinking about catching a bug," said Number Three.

"Right now?" said Frog, who was known to be congenial and cooperative.

"Sure," said Number Three. "Go ahead and show me your technique, and let me see what happens."

"Okay," said Frog, and he looked up, and just then a grasshopper leaped from the bank and flew right over his head and Frog snapped at it and missed.

"Well, what happened?" asked Number Three. "I see you missed."

"Thinking didn't work at all," said Frog. "When the grasshopper was flying over me just then, I thought about the grasshopper flying over me just then, and about making sure that I had the right position and angle to strike from, and then completing my precise tongue-snap, from start to finish, and then snagging my prey in mid-flight."

"And what happened?" said Number Three.

"By the time I thought about all of the details," Frog said, "the grasshopper was gone."

"And so, you're right," said Number Three. "Thinking about catching insects when you're catching them really doesn't work so well for you, if at all, does it?"

"True, but not really," said Frog.

"Well then, why do you teach all of the techniques to your students," said Number Three, "if the techniques aren't useful to them?"

"I *do* teach all of the techniques that I've learned over the years, and they *are* useful to my students. But I'm always telling them, 'when a bug appears, forget everything you've learned and just go after it.'"

"So, you teach your students how to catch bugs," said Number Three, "and then tell them to forget what they've been taught?"

"That's right, more or less," said Frog. "And wrong too. I mean—it works pretty well. After all, how can you catch bugs unless you've mastered the techniques of catching bugs? I'm here to teach my students how to do it…otherwise—" (his voice seemed to drift away on a sudden breeze rippling across The Pond).

"So that's what you mean about thinking and not thinking?" said Number Three.

"To put it another way," said Frog, "it's more like *both this and that.* That's why my young students must listen and watch carefully when I teach them, and then be ready to forget everything they've learned when it comes time to snatch a bug out of the air and eat, in order to go on living."

"What you're saying sort of makes sense by not making sense," said Number Three.

"And aren't you saying the same thing about your maze-running?" said Frog. "You've learned all of the techniques, and can even perform them in your mind. But then you can just take off and run through that maze without anything in your mind, and even have a quicker maze time. Isn't that true?"

"Yes, that's true," said Number Three. Then he thanked Frog for his comments, said goodbye and left. About fifteen seconds later, Number Three turned around and saw Frog snap at something over his head. He was too far away to know if the attempt was a success.

It was later that same day that Number Three decided that he no longer wanted to be one of The Five, because it meant having to agree to be merely a part of something much bigger than himself, something that he had no control over. He was tired of the rat-step pace to his life, and especially tired of having to cooperate in a hunt to destroy animals every day just to fulfill a quota. He longed for the day when he could separate himself from the others and go on his own, and do what he himself wanted to do, just because he wanted to do it, and at his own pace.

And so, another one of Number Three's secrets was that in spite of having to lead a confined and regimented life right now, and moving in the too-slow-for-him-pace of the pack, he could, at the same time, look forward to another way to live. And he could also, in the meantime, be free, at least in his mind.

15: Maze Momentum

That same night, after hours at The Maze, Number Three heard another familiar voice just as he emerged from The End: "What's this I hear about you acting up in this maze?" Though it was dark, there was a full moon that provided enough light to see into The Maze. Number Three stood at attention. "Well, sir—"

"Relax," said Sniff.

"Yeah, sir," said Number Three, breathing fairly hard. "It's just that going through The Maze is so easy for me, and I hate to go slow, and—"

"Yeah, you hate it alright," said Sniff, sniffing, "you hate it enough to disrupt the training sessions."

"I don't mean to, sir," said Number Three.

"What's your best time so far?" said Sniff.

"Two minutes and twenty-two seconds, sir," said Number Three.

"Two minutes and twenty-two seconds!" Sniff's eyes were bulged up, and he sniffed.

"Yeah, sir," said Number Three.

"How come the two twenty-two is not posted as the record," said Sniff. "The record is four-sixteen."

"Well, sir," said Number Three, "Stub told me that my time is just too fast to be posted as official, since nobody else's time comes anywhere near it, and so it might discourage others from coming to The Maze, let alone to try to break my record."

"How come you're so fast?" said Sniff.

"Maybe because I've always had fast legs," said Number Three. "And of course, practice. I've been doing a lot of practicing."

"I want you to show me your speed," said Sniff, looking down at Number Three's muscular legs.

"Sir?"

"Go around there to The Beginning and when you hear me say 'Go, Go.' I want to time you myself."

"Yeah, sir," said Number Three, and he took off and ran around The Maze and stood at The Beginning, crouched, ready. When he heard *Go!* he shot through the passages like a rat on fire and burst through The End, just as Sniff punched his stop-button.

"Two minutes and twelve seconds—I'll be a—how do you *do* that?" said Sniff, studying his watch.

"Speed, sir; fast legs. But I work hard, too. I intend to get my time down to what I think it can be—maybe a minute and a half."

"Tell me, what're you thinking about when you go through that maze—do you have The Way memorized so well that you just tell yourself what the turns are, as you go?"

"Not exactly, sir," said Number Three. He was for the first time in his life fairly comfortable speaking to Sniff, who had always made him feel apprehensive. But of course, Number Three was talking about what he knew better than anyone else in The Woods.

"What's it like, running through there; what's it feel like; what's in your head?" asked Sniff.

"Well, sir," said Number Three, "I had to learn the technique of running, and get it all down in my head and body."

"Technique?" said Sniff. "What's technique got to do with it?"

"Well, sir, just in a few runs I learned to shift my feet and turn my body at full speed and lean into the turns. I've learned all the angles and the steps and I've locked them up in my memory, and in my body, all the angles and moves, perfectly."

Sniff looked at Number Three's muscular legs again.

"The Way gets into you," said Number Three.

"Okay, how about me—can you make me into a great maze-runner?" asked Sniff.

"Sir, you need to practice a lot."

"Okay," said Sniff. "Can you show me, right now, some of that so-called technique?"

"Yeah, okay, sir," said Number Three. The two walked around to the front of The Maze. Moonlight shone into The Beginning.

"Now, the first thing," said Number Three, "is timing. You gotta hit all the turns exactly right, exactly at the right time. And you need to be always looking straight ahead, right down the middle of The Way—I mean, splitting the dark. Pretend that you've got a second tail sticking right out of your nose, straight out, and aim right over that tail. You're sighting, but it's not so much sighting as smelling.

You need to *smell* that path, The Way. I call it *nose-tailing*. Now when you get in there, the first thing you do is take two quick steps to your left, and one step to your right, then four steps straight ahead. But you need to be leaning a little right when you do it because the next move—"

"Okay," said Sniff, looking a little puzzled. "I'm ready."

"And one more thing," said Number Three.

"What's that?" asked Sniff, crouched, and ready to go.

"Breathing," said Number Three.

"Breathing?"

"Yeah, sir, everything depends on your breathing. When you're making a move that's really crucial, you need to be exhaling; and when you—"

"Wait a minute, I'm always breathing. What's this breathing stuff?" said Sniff.

"It comes from the center of your body," said Number Three. "It's called center point."

"Forget the center point, I just want to see what I can do," said Sniff.

"Okay," said Number Three, "When I say *go*, do everything I told you to do. And don't forget—starts are everything. Good beginnings create momentum: Maze Momentum, I call it."

"I'm ready," said Sniff.

"Okay," said Number Three. "Get set! (Sniff was squinting straight into The Maze) Go!" Sniff took two steps inside and fell on his nose, bounced up, turned right, hit the wall, bounced off, turned to his right again, fell again, caught himself going down, stumbled once more, and fell again. This time he stayed down.

"Get me outta here!" he yelled at Number Three, who ran through the entrance and helped him to his feet, and led him out of The Beginning.

"What happened?" said Sniff, holding his sore nose.

"Sir, you must've turned the wrong way on that first move," said Number Three. "Your posture was looking good, and then—"

"I don't understand it," said Sniff. "I'm the same animal you are. Look at me: four legs, a thin tail, teeth for gnawing, a good mind for mazes, same as you, same as all rats. What's my problem?"

"Well, sir, you have to give it some time, and a lot of work," said Number Three. "And maybe you're not naturally as fast as some rats—I mean, maybe it's partly genetics, I don't know for sure."

"Yeah, sure," said Sniff, and he turned around and walked away on shaky legs, rubbing his aching nose, and sniffing.

The very next day Sniff designated Number Three as Maze Pro and Manager. From now on his job would be teaching and training. He would be replaced on The Five by another able rat, so that group would still be intact. Number Three, however, was not happy that his replacement would be called by the same name, but his new job title—especially the word "pro"—made the change worthwhile. He knew that the original four of The Five wouldn't miss him, since lately he could tell they'd begun to think of him as being both literally and figuratively out of step, as well as somewhat conceited.

Stub would still be collecting running, spectator, and violations fees, as well as those from lessons taught by Number Three. He very much disliked his demotion from manager status, and he was still secretly upset with Sniff for not giving him credit for his maze dream.

That same night, Sniff had Number Three guide him through The Maze. When they emerged from The End, Sniff had him change the record sign. Now it said:

THE MAZE RECORD:
2 Minutes, 42 Seconds—SNIFF

"You know how it goes," Sniff said to Number Three, "The boss's gotta always have the record." Then he winked. "Otherwise, it looks bad." The wink, Number Three assumed, meant that Sniff knew that he was only the official record holder, and that the *actual* record-holder was The Maze Pro—the one that Sniff was talking to.

"Yeah, sir," said Number Three, and he half-smiled, going along with the wink.

"Besides," Sniff went on, "all of us rats should share the record equally, since we're all the same animal. Right?"

"Well, sir," said Number Three, "we *could* just post the records as Rat Maze Records, couldn't we?" He had surprised himself by asking such an audacious question, which was also fairly sarcastic, and whose answer he hoped would be negative.

"We could do that," said Sniff, "but the animals expect their leader to be the best."

"I see your point, sir," said Number Three (immediately regretting that he had given into Sniff's assertion of authority so easily).

"And by the way," Sniff went on, "would you mind slowing down a little on your maze runs, so you don't look like you're beating my record?"

"No problem, sir," said Number Three (once more, feeling some regret). At that moment, Number Three began to realize that, although he knew in his heart that he was the very fastest maze runner of The Woods—and that most of the animals, at least the ones who were observant and curious, and cared for facts, and for the truth, also knew it—he'd still have to live with Sniff's lie.

That night, just before he fell asleep, Number Three was thinking that living in The Woods, after all, meant having to put with a lot of stuff an animal didn't necessarily want to have to put up with.

16: Prove It

Ever since his first exasperating attempt at maze-running on Opening Day, Claws had made sure he kept improving by going back for more runs daily, both before and after work. Though he had figured out The Way and was steadily improving on his time, he was having to constantly fight his instinct to leap up and over the walls during his runs. Not only that, but he was also being slowed down (as if by an invisible force), whenever his run was going very well. He had mentioned to Number Three his feelings about these things (as well as the ongoing annoyance of having to see the squirrel tail on a stick at the end of every run). Number Three's response was that the sensation of being tripped up was "probably due to a lively imagination." Of course, Number Three was aware of Sniff's vigilante trippers, but had decided it would be futile to challenge him on the matter, knowing his response would be anything but positive.

Claws also joined a new group, The Anti-Rules League (ARL), which was opposed to some of the rules of The Maze. Besides himself, the other initial members were two other squirrels, a mink, a blackbird, a dove, and three sparrows. At the group's first meeting, there was unanimous agreement that Claws should become a candidate for the leader of The Woods. Claws said he had not yet even thought about being a candidate and running against Sniff, with whom (as many in the group already knew) he had had strong disagreements in the past—but that he would definitely give it some thought.

Claws burst out of The End on an early morning run and the timer yelled out his time—"three thirty one"—and on his way back to The Beginning for another run, he heard the familiar, shrill, high-pitched voice of Sniff, who was standing close by: "Three-thirty-one—is that the best you can do?"

"Is that a serious question?" said Claws, breathing hard, "or are you just bragging about your record?"

Sniff sniffed, then snickered. "Just thought I'd ask," he said. "I've heard that you're over here practicing every day, morning and evening."

"Yeah, I'm here a lot," said Claws, still breathing hard, "and by the way, why is it that whenever I see you at The Maze, whatever time of the day, I never ever see you doing any maze-running?" The long, wordy question made Claws gasp, and rescue his breath.

"I don't need to do any maze runs," said Sniff. "I already have the record, as I'm sure you've noticed many times."

"Yes, I've noticed," said Claws, "but tell me—about how many times have you run this maze?"

"Only once," answered Sniff.

"Really?" said Claws, finally breathing normally. "So you're telling me that you ran this maze only one time and you're the official record holder?"

"You got it," said Sniff.

"Tell me," said Claws, "how come you're so fast?"

"First of all," said Sniff, "leaders, like me, are faster than followers, like you. That's due to genetics—natural athletic ability, great foot speed, and a great maze mind."

"In other words, you're a natural, huh?" said Claws.

"That's right," said Sniff. "And my center point is excellent too."

"Really?" said Claws.

"And my nose-tailing technique's not bad either," said Sniff.

"Really?" said Claws (who was also familiar with Number Three's maze terminology).

"For sure," said Sniff, sniffing.

"Okay, then," said Claws, "if you're so fast, why don't you go ahead and prove it—just get in there and do a run."

"I don't need to prove it," said Sniff. "I already did prove it. The record is posted near The Beginning."

"Don't you want to improve on your record?" asked Claws. "Aren't you worried that somebody might come along and break it?"

"Do I look worried?" said Sniff.

"You ever hear the expression," said Claws, "practice makes perfect?"

"I have," said Sniff, "but I don't see how it can apply to me."

"Well, I'm practicing every day," said Claws. "Every single day."

"I'm afraid," said Sniff, "that you squirrels just don't have it in you to set a maze record. That takes a leader, in other words, an all-around athlete."

"I suppose you consider yourself the all-around best athlete in The Woods. Right?" said Claws.

"You know any animal who's a better all-around animal, physically and mentally—than the one you're talking to?"

"You mean also the best climber?" said Claws.

Sniff laughed. "I don't do much climbing," he said, "but if I turned my attention to it, I'm sure I could hold my own against anybody, including you."

"Is that right?" said Claws. "And how about leaping? I suppose you're the best leaper too?"

"If and when I turn my attention to it, absolutely," said Sniff.

"Then why don't we have a little climbing contest on The Oak?" said Claws.

"Let me tell you something," said Sniff. "Leaders don't waste their time and energy climbing trees."

"Well," said Claws, "anytime you'd like to have a little tree race, just say so. And that goes for leaping too. You know where I live."

"Yeah, I know where you live—in my tree," said Sniff.

"*Your* tree?" said Claws, his eyes enlarging, his face suddenly beginning to feel warm.

"That's right," said Sniff. "*My* tree. The tree of the leader of The Woods."

"You? The leader of The Woods?" said Claws. "I thought that was Owl."

"Not for long," said Sniff. "He's retiring soon—remember?"

By now Claws' face was hot, and as red as his fur. He turned around abruptly, swished his tail until it stood straight out, and scampered away to the first tree he came to and climbed it quickly to the very top branch, which could barely hold his muscular body. He stayed there for several minutes—balancing, swaying slightly, and chattering. Then when his face had lost its heat, he climbed down and found a piece of bark, which he took to his nest, and wrote a poem on. Then he hung it on a branch close to his nest. The poem said:

GET OUT OF MY FACE,
GET OFF OF MY CASE,
THIS IS MY PLACE
Claws

17: "Closed for Repairs"

That same day The Maze was closed from noon until late into the evening. Spider (with a new blueprint), Stub and The Five, six more rats and six more moles (with Sniff looking on and constantly commenting), constructed a new Way by dismantling and then expanding The Maze's walls on one side, so that there would now be two different maze routes. The first maze-route would be unchanged, and called, on a new sign near The Beginning, "The Easy Way." The new maze-route—with twice as many turns and dead ends as in the first route—would be called, on a sign near The Beginning, "The Hard Way." The new route would cost seventy-five cents. Now Spider would have a total of twelve webs for snagging her prey.

Late in the evening, another phase of work was completed, this one without Spider. The project—a dimly lit secret tunnel, which Sniff called "a repair tunnel"—was another one of Stub's ideas from a dream, appropriated by Sniff, who claimed to have had a similar dream. Two trap doors were installed inside the Hard Way, one just inside The Beginning and one just inside The End. All an animal had to do was to enter The Beginning, turn left into a dead-end, grab a cleverly concealed handle on the floor, drop down underground, close the door over his head, travel the length of The Maze, lift another cleverly concealed handle, climb into another dead-end, take a right turn, and emerge upward and out through The End. All of the workers on this project were sworn to secrecy. Just after the project was finished, it occurred to Stub what the tunnel was for.

"Aren't you breaking one of the rules of The Maze?" he asked Sniff.

"Which rule are you referring to?" said Sniff.

"The one that says 'no cheating,'" said Stub.

"There's no rule that says you can't run *underneath* The Maze, is there?" said Sniff, sniffing, then winking.

"But isn't it still cheating?" said Stub.

"Well," said Sniff, "everybody knows that the ones who *make* the rules are never the cheaters. It's always the ones who are supposed to *follow* the rules who do the cheating."

Stub was silent for a moment, then said: "You know, in my dream, it really *was* a repair tunnel."

Sniff, in a hurry to leave, mentioned a bonus for Stub for "all of your great community work." Stub said he appreciated the compliment, which sounded sincere to him, and the extra money, and that was the end of the conversation.

One more sign was set on a tripod near The Beginning. It said:

NOTICE: STARTING IMMEDIATELY:
DAILY HARD WAY EXHIBITION RUNS
BY SNIFF (ONLY 50 CENTS!)

18: Respect vs. Affection

On a branch, reading, Butterfly closed her book when she looked up and saw Wing approaching. He landed softly, so as not to perturb her delicate wings, they greeted each other, and he said, "I've got some more good questions for you today."

"I always appreciate your questions," said Butterfly.

"That makes me glad," said Wing. "For a start, do you agree with me that probably the luckiest trait an animal can possess is curiosity?"

"I do agree," said Butterfly.

"And that the opposite of death is not life, but curiosity?" said Wing.

"That makes sense," said Butterfly, "because if you lose your curiosity, what's left for you?"

"And now here's another question for you," said Wing. "Which is more important, when it comes to interacting with another animal—respect or affection?"

"I'd say affection," said Butterfly, "because, although it's also important to respect others, if you don't like another animal, your respect for them may turn sour."

"But if you don't really like them in the first place," said Wing, "why should you have respect for them?"

"Because all of us live in The Woods together," said Butterfly, "and we need to get along. Just because you don't like someone doesn't mean they don't deserve your respect."

"Respect is easier to come by than affection, isn't it?" said Wing.

"Yes," said Butterfly, "you can't *will* affection, but you can, to an extent, will respect. But friendship is a gift."

"That's right," said Wing. "True friendship needs no explanation. It soars on its own wings, stands on its own feet. And yet I keep wondering: should we, can we, truly respect Sniff?"

"Yes," said Butterfly. "We can at least have respect for him. But you're an individualist. Why do you need to do anything, or agree with anybody on anything, if you don't want to?"

"It's more complicated than that," said Wing. "I do see your point about respecting others, if for no other reason than that we want them to respect us."

"For the sake of the community, then?" said Butterfly.

Wing shifted a little on the branch to be more comfortable. "I'd say as Frog would say: 'Yes/no,'" he said.

"Meaning?" said Butterfly.

"Yes, for the sake of the community," Wing said. "And no, because individuals come first. After all, if there's no individuals around, there's no community."

"You like to bring everything back to the individual, don't you?" said Butterfly.

"Maybe I can't help it," said Wing. "But let me ask you another question, which is a variation on the last question I asked."

"Go ahead," said Butterfly.

"Should we actually respect an evil animal like Sniff?" said Wing.

"But aren't we talking about evil acts and not evil animals?" said Butterfly. "We're all capable of committing bad if not downright evil acts, so if we lose respect for a single animal among us, doesn't that mean that none of the rest of us deserve respect?"

"But couldn't Sniff's evil acts, because they're so plentiful and atrocious, be an exception to your argument?" said Wing.

"I don't think so," said Butterfly. "My point is that if we don't have respect for others, we might as well throw away all rules and all decency in The Woods. And besides, Sniff has some positive traits."

"Positive traits?" said Wing. "For example?"

"He looks out for his own kind," said Butterfly, "and he can get things done."

"But we all look after our own kind," said Wing. "And don't you agree that we can't allow him to be our leader?"

"Yes, we can't allow that," said Butterfly.

"But how will we ever stop him?" asked Wing.

"We have to somehow persuade him that his destructive actions have no place in The Woods," said Butterfly.

"He's so clever," said Wing. "He's already got a huge contingent of animals believing in him, and not just rats— plenty of other four-legged ones, like squirrels, and all kinds of winged animals as well. So many votes, who could ever beat him in an election? And he's having The Five kill off so many animals—including some of his own believers who don't happen to be rats—every day." Wing paused, took a deep breath and went on: "I'm thinking that the only way you can deal with a Sniff is to eliminate him altogether—or should I say, e-rat-icate him."

"I would never agree to that," said Butterfly.

"You do realize, don't you," said Wing, "that Sniff will not stop until he conquers The Woods."

"I believe he'd like to be the ruler," said Butterfly.

"But you're right," said Wing. "And of course, we have to try to encourage as many animals as we can not to vote for him. Something's got to be done to stop that rat."

"I think we can do it," said Butterfly, fluttering her wings.

"Now here's another idea that might be useful to us," said Wing. "Might there be a way to find out what goes on inside Sniff's head? Is it possible to understand the actual machinery churning in that brain of his? How can any of us become better animals unless we know what we're really like, *as animals*?"

"I like your idea," said Butterfly. "Why not consult with that well-known brain scientist, The Crow, from The Isle of Crows?"

"Say, now that is an excellent idea," said Wing, shifting his position on the branch and lifting his head in an optimistic gesture.

"The Crow sees a lot of dead animals," said Butterfly, "and so he must be well informed about brains, and therefore, animal behavior."

"Yes," said Wing, "in other words, he picks their brains and eats the pickings. Maybe it's time to pick The Crow's brain."

"That's a good way to put it," said Butterfly. "Everybody knows that he flies on the same route through The Woods several days every week."

"Yes, I believe usually early in the morning," said Wing. "He used to live in The Woods and still has a lot of friends here."

"That's what I heard too," said Butterfly. "Let's try to intercept him the next time he comes through, and consult with him."

"Why don't you have the conversation with him," said Wing. "We could do it together, but since hawks compete with crows for food, I think you would get along better with him. And we can, of course, split the fee."

"Of course," said Butterfly.

"Alright," said Wing. "I'm looking forward to learning something. When shall we two meet again?"

"Let's say when the leaves are falling faster," said Butterfly, who opened her book just as Wing said, "Yes," opened his wings and quickly traded the branch for the sky.

19: The Dream Machine

"What do you dream about?" Sniff asked Spider. It was a beautiful, crisp, fall day, with leaves displaying colors from brown to red to yellow beginning, sporadically, to come down.

"Quite often my dreams are about webs," said Spider.

"Webs?" said Sniff.

"Yes," said Spider. "Making webs, fixing them, especially catching bugs in them."

"Let me tell you about a dream I've been having a lot lately," said Sniff (actually, it was another dream of Stub's). "In my dream, I'm inside The Hole. Right in front of me, there's a machine with a large screen, and on the screen is a picture of The Woods. Under the screen, there's a keyboard with hundreds of keys on it."

"The Woods are on the screen?" said Spider.

"Yes," said Sniff. "All of it—every animal, every leaf, every tree, every bush and flower and blade of grass, and weed. Everything is happening that happens in The Woods, and it's all happening just as I'm watching it—all at the present time. Feeding, escaping, flying, leaping, hiding, mating, giving birth, protecting the newborn, sneaking around, attacking, getting attacked, getting old, getting sick, dying—all of it, everything."

"What a strange dream," said Spider, her six little eyes glimmering with attention.

"But what's *really* strange is what happens if I push some keys on the keyboard," said Sniff.

"And what happens then?" asked Spider.

"When I push the keys, things begin to change," said Sniff. "For example, when I push one of them, everything begins to go dark, like at night. Another row of keys brings the seasons—spring, summer, fall, winter—another row of keys brings morning, and light. Another row brings fire, another one brings rain, another one, snow. I can push keys that make the snowflakes start to come down softly, or so thick and heavy that they begin to fill up The Woods. And some keys are for wind. I push them and leaves and branches begin to move, and if I push other keys the branches begin to bend, even break off, and scatter all over the ground. I can make the weather bleak, full of a violent, howling wind, from any direction. And when I keep pushing other keys, I can bring torrential rain, or a tornado, or a blizzard. A single key can bring up bright sunlight winking through the trees. Another key can send a single leaf, or a thousand, to the ground. Thousands and thousands even—or just like the way they're coming down today—a few at a time. Just by pushing keys."

"That's quite a dream," said Spider.

"Or, with other keys," said Sniff, "I can bring a calm day with no wind. I can bring whatever month I want to bring, and make everything grow; I can bring the odors of spring, the new colors, and the sounds, like the chirping of robins in the spring, or the rasping sound of cicadas in the fall."

"Really?" said Spider.

"And not only that," said Sniff. "I can push keys in another row and change the animals."

"What do you mean, 'change the animals'?" asked Spider.

"These other keys allow me to select certain animals," said Sniff. "If I push one of them, all the fish in The Pond come up, the screen is full of water, with fins flashing all over. Or a row of keys for porcupines, all the porcupines at once if I want to, or minks, or birds, or chipmunks. And I can bring up any single animal too. Then I can change that animal by pushing other keys."

"How's that?" asked Spider.

"I can chase it away, make it sit still, even knock it down if I want to," said Sniff.

"Knock it down?" asked Spider.

"If I push one of the other keys," said Sniff, "the animal gets hit with a powerful force. And if it's hit in a vulnerable spot on its body, it goes down. And I can make it stay down, and never get up again."

"What a frightening thing to see," said Spider.

"But here's the strangest part of all," said Sniff.

"What's that?" said Spider.

"There's other keys, too, and these keys are even more specific."

"What do you mean?"

"I mean I can bring up any particular animal," said Sniff, "like Fox, or Frog, or any animal you could name. And I can bring up you if I want to."

"And in this dream that you keep dreaming," said Spider, "have you tried all of the keys?"

"No. At least not yet," said Sniff. "There's way too many keys to try them all, and the dream always ends too soon, anyway."

"And are you disappointed that you can't try all of the keys, or at least most of them?" asked Spider.

"Sure, I am," said Sniff.

"And how do you feel about that dream?" asked Spider.

"It's fascinating," said Sniff. "I like it a lot."

"Why?" said Spider.

"Because I can make The Woods do whatever I want," said Sniff. "All I have to do is push the keys. I can change anything I want to change, and make things better than they were before I changed them. I wish I had a machine like that. If I could have that machine—a real one and not one in a dream—I could change The Woods in a few hours, or maybe no more than a day, or a few days."

"But isn't that too much influence and control for one animal to have?" asked Spider.

"The Woods need changing, I can tell you that," said Sniff.

"But you would be the only animal that has the power to change it?" said Spider.

"It might as well be me," said Sniff.

"And why is that—why you?" said Spider.

"Because I know what needs to be done with The Woods, but I don't yet know how to do it," said Sniff. His look was serious, dark. His whiskers were twitching as he sniffed.

"Well," said Spider, "I know I wouldn't want to have all that influence. And I don't think any other animal in The Woods should have that much influence either."

"But wouldn't you like to be able to trap all of the bugs you needed for the rest of your life?" asked Sniff.

"What do you mean?" said Spider.

"I mean," said Sniff, "you could call up all the bugs on the screen, stop them right there, and then go get them. It would be so easy for you."

"Yes, but—it's not the natural way," said Spider.

"What's the difference, as long as you can eat?" said Sniff.

"I don't know for sure, but I like life the way it is," said Spider. "Even if it isn't perfect."

"But what if you could design a machine like that?" said Sniff.

"Are you crazy?" said Spider. "Even if I *could* design such a machine—and it's way beyond my expertise—I wouldn't do it."

"Why not?" asked Sniff.

"I wouldn't do it for the reason I gave you," said Spider. "I don't think any of us, whoever we are, should have the right to use such a machine."

"There is no possibility that you would change your mind and at least give it a try?" asked Sniff.

"You are an ambitious animal, aren't you?" said Spider.

"Maybe I am," said Sniff, "but I know a machine like that could do a lot of good in The Woods."

"Should any one animal have the right to decide what's good and what's bad?" asked Spider. "And if so, who should it be?"

"Me," said Sniff, and with that word, the conversation was over, and Sniff turned around and left.

20: Two Lives

"What's it like to be able to fly?" Claws asked Wing. The two were sitting on a branch in the middle of cottonwood. Claws noticed that just asking a question made it easy to talk when he really wanted to know something, especially when he was talking to an animal that he liked, and who was highly respected.

"It's a feeling that's hard to describe," said Wing, "but maybe you know a little about it because you yourself sometimes come close to flying, don't you?"

"Yes, sometimes when I leap from one tree to another," said Claws, "it feels like I'm close to flying. But it's still only a leap, it's not quite flying."

"Why do you leap from tree to tree and almost fly, when it's so dangerous?" asked Wing.

"Mainly to get wherever I'm going quicker," said Claws.

"That's one good thing about flying," said Wing.

"But what's it like being up there in the sky and just flying around?" asked Claws.

"It's a strange/familiar feeling, as Frog might say," said Wing. "A well-known eagle once put it well in a poem: flying feels like 'being free in my loneliness and lonely in my freedom.'"

"I don't quite get that," said Claws, "and yet I do get it, more or less. I can feel completely free when I leap, for a second or two, but I've always got a branch in front of me that I have to find so I won't fall."

"That must be one thing that's different between leaping and flying," said Wing. "When you leap you always leap toward a goal, another branch, or the ground. And yet I too have a goal in mind when I'm flying, but it's not necessarily an immediate goal."

"Tell me more," said Claws.

"When I fly, I don't need to go anywhere in particular," said Wing. "I can just fly, and yet, like you, I can have a goal in mind, even if that goal is not a conscious one."

"What do you mean?" said Claws.

"Well, it's like this," said Wing. "I'm a hunter, so I'm always looking for something to eat, and I of course hunt as I fly. But what I eventually find I can't see or know about until I find it while I'm in the air flying. 'On the wing,' as we birds like to say."

"That's making a little more sense," said Claws.

"Let me try to explain further," said Wing. "I fly around high above The Woods and the meadows and the animals. The animals I feed on know that I'm up there above them, somewhere, and I know they are down there below me, somewhere. I fly around, bolstered by air and a breeze or wind; I'm just flying as if only for the sake of flying. But then when something catches my eye, a very strange feeling comes over me. The pure feeling of flying changes to another feeling, but this other feeling is not a feeling with freedom in it. It's actually the opposite of freedom. Suddenly I'm confined, imprisoned, locked inside the need to attack and capture in my talons whatever it is that has caught my eye. Maybe it's a rabbit, a mouse, or maybe just a slight, quick ripple of wind on the grass."

"I can see that this other feeling is very different from the first one of just flying around," said Claws.

"Yes," said Wing. "The very instant my eyesight fixes on something, my wings begin to take me there. I'm seized by this need to swoop down on it, to catch it before it gets away."

"So, there's two parts to your flying," said Claws (who just then pictured himself being seized by a big hawk or eagle).

"Yes. The first part I'm talking about is more or less conscious," said Wing. "I can fly wherever I want to fly, and I enjoy that part of flying very much: to soar, to climb, to ride the wind in any direction I want and for as long as I want. And then there's the second part, which is pretty much unconscious, which comes after I see something moving below me. But both parts belong to flying. I have to be free at first, in order to discover, to see. And then that freedom leads to the part that I can't control, the part in which I'm no longer free."

"It must feel strange," said Claws.

"It *does* feel strange," said Wing.

"Is there anything else you can tell me about flying?" said Claws.

"At least one more thing," said Wing. "But maybe it's just another way of saying what I've already said."

"And what's that?" asked Claws.

"Flying is *my* way," said Wing. "I would not be what I am without wings."

"That makes sense," said Claws.

Wing shifted on the branch. "Now it's your turn to tell me what it's like to be a squirrel," he said.

"I too have a double life," said Claws. "One is on the ground, the other is in trees. Just like you, I like to be up high, to see from above. You have a bird's eye view of things; I have a squirrel's eye view of things. Leaves and branches can be my sky. And they can hide me from what's below, or above, that may harm me. On the ground, I'm mainly a hider. My feet are light and quick, and I hide things in secret places. My life on the ground is a secret, which I'm always trying to hide. To escape, for me, to avoid danger, is to rise. Up-ness is what I need to stay alive. And when I have to flee, I have claws. If one tree can't take me high enough, I rise or shoot out level to find another tree that'll take me higher yet, or several trees, however many it takes to lift me up to where I need to go.

"My life is a life of touch, of touch and go. I feel it best in my sharp claws, my head above or below that sharpness, upside down or right-side up, it makes no difference. Like you birds, I know up from down, and prefer up. I often dream of rising higher and higher. I also dream of the sound and the feel of my claws on rough bark. The ground is for running on, for chasing other squirrels and then suddenly being chased by them in the opposite direction. The ground is for hiding things, including myself. I escape one moment so I can live the whole next day. I need to stay sharp-eyed; I need to be accurate with my claws. When I leap, I know what I'm leaping from and into or onto. I look before I leap, because if I miss, I may never leap again. Just one mistake and—and—"

Claws stopped, he had run out of words. His heart was beating fast, his claws were tense, his eyes wide open. He had clicked off his words faster than his claws going up a tree—even his words had claw marks on them.

"That's a marvelous life," said Wing, "and you describe it like a true poet. You've given it some thought, haven't you?"

"Yes," said Claws, "I've got a lot of time to think, up in my nest."

At that point in the conversation, Claws began to have another thought, and he noticed how his mind seemed to still be running up a tree or across the ground as fast as a squirrel can go. "But I have a strange dream," he said. "I have it often."

"And what is your dream about?" asked Wing.

"It's a dream of hiding my words in the ground, and then digging them up later."

"I wonder what that dream means," said Wing.

"I don't know what it means," said Claws, "but that's my dream."

"I think it's the dream of a poet," said Wing.

"It might be," said Claws. "Words are secrets, maybe. Is that what you mean?"

"I like the idea," said Wing. "Words as secrets."

"It's as if I hide my words and then dig them up later," Claws said, "so I can find out what I said."

"That's a good way to describe how poems are made," said Wing. "First, you bury the words, as if they're a treasure, and then you dig them up, and that's the poem—that's what you had to say."

"That's it; that's right," said Claws. "Maybe not exactly, but it's close to what I'm trying to get at."

When Claws thanked Wing for the good conversation, Wing became effusive. "Thank you," he said. "I appreciate the good, honest talk. Let's do it again sometime."

Claws agreed, and he climbed down the tree and started for home, as Wing was flying away.

21: The Kingdom of Sharing

The crowd for Owl's next-to-last Appearance was somewhat larger than usual—more rats, for instance, and more birds and squirrels. Frog was there, as usual, as were Stub, Spider, the Possums, Claws, and Number Three. As was their habit, Wing and Butterfly were perched on a branch.

After the four (of The Five) took up the collection for the Oak Restoration Fund, the first speaker, Number Two, directed the crowd's attention to Sniff, who was standing behind them and just outside The Beginning of The Hard Way—crouched and ready to go. "Animals of The Woods," said Number Two, "this run will be Sniff's first exhibition run on the day of an Appearance, which makes it quite special. Sniff considers his run to be a great contribution to the community, and therefore, it's free of charge."

At the timer's "Go!" Sniff lurched inside, stepped into the dead end, and lifted the trapdoor. He, of course, could afford to go the length of the tunnel at a slow pace (even for a slow animal), so that his time wouldn't seem outrageously fast. When he emerged from The End, the timer shouted, "one minute, sixteen seconds—a new record!" Sniff raised a paw to acknowledge the crowd's rousing burst of applause. On his way back to The Hole, Number Two spoke again:

"Animals of The Woods, don't forget: This record by Sniff is not an Easy Way record, it's a *Hard Way* record. We all know that it takes a super athlete to set such a fast record."

Now there was some talking among the animals, as they waited for Owl to come out of The Hole: "Look," said one mole to another, pointing at Sniff, "he's not even breathing hard—what a great runner!"

Claws, who was close by, overheard the comment. "One minute, sixteen seconds?" he said. "That's not sounding right to me."

"Have you been running The Hard Way yet, Claws?" asked a mink.

"Every day," said Claws. "Morning and night."

"I hear you're really fast too," said a rabbit.

"Thank you," said Claws. "My times are going down."

Owl finally stepped out onto The Big Limb, was handed the microphone by Number Two, who then stepped into The Hole. Owl looked out and down at the audience.

"My dooooooooootiful fellow animals," he said, "it is yooooooooooo who have shown great fortitoooooooooood in your dooooooooootiful efforts against Fox. It is yooooooooooo who have shown great fortitoooooooooood. It is yooooooooooo who have kept us from constant attack from Fox. I thank yooooooooo for your dooooooooootiful efforts, your dooooooooootiful efforts." He set his microphone down, took his three famous steps, dropped off the limb into the air, plummeted straight down like a big white stone and all at once, just as the ground was about to meet him, opened his wings, swooped grandly over the heads of the animals—who felt the warm, familiar wash of wings and heard the familiar clattering—then rose and circled above the crowd once, twice, and swooped low, nearly scraping the ground with a wing; then, as the cheering and applause increased, disappeared into the trees, just as Sniff stepped out of The Hole onto The Big Limb, picked up the microphone, and, as usual, raising a paw and smiling, accepted the applause as his own.

Now looking down at the happy, up-turned faces, he calmed the audience with a raised paw, and put the microphone to his whiskers. "My fellow animals of The Woods," he said, "no animal has ever surpassed my maze-time in the past—in either The Easy Way or The Hard Way. And no animal will ever surpass my maze-time in the future—except me. Isn't that true?" Sniff got plenty of applause for the comment, gesturing for more and more applause, and when it died down, he smiled and went on: "I have some special news for you today. It has to do with a special event that will take place next Friday at Owl's last Appearance."

"We're all dying to hear the special news," yelled Wing, who then quickly flew to a branch close to The Big Limb, and Sniff, feeling the small wind from Wing's approach and landing, moved a couple of steps in the opposite direction.

"But first," said Sniff, looking at Wing, and then down at the crowd, "I've got some questions for our famous, feathered po-et."

"I'm still listening," said Wing (as they talked, both looked sometimes at the crowd and sometimes at each other).

"Here's my first question," said Sniff. "Why hasn't our beloved Po-et of The Woods composed a po-em about our great leader, Owl, and made a public reading of it from The Big Limb?"

"I don't tend to write or recite poems unless I feel inclined," said Wing. "Question number two?"

"That's interesting," said Sniff. "And here's another question. Why haven't you, our distinguished po-et-with-wings, taken advantage of our new, wonderful recreation, The Maze?" Sniff's question this time brought a brief burst of applause.

"The Maze was designed for ground animals," said Wing, "especially rats like you."

"I've heard that you're pretty graceful," said Sniff, who looked upward. "At least in the sky (Sniff smiled, and sniffed). I would assume that you'd enjoy trying to figure out 'The Way of The Maze'—I mean, of course, '*The Easy Way* of The Maze' (he smiled again)."

"I've got more important things to figure out these days," said Wing. "But why don't you get on with your so-called special news."

"Well," said Sniff, "in fact, our brief conversation here is a fitting lead-in to my special news."

"Go ahead," said Wing.

"Next Friday, as you all know," said Sniff, "will be Owl's last Appearance. You all know as well that Owl has selected me to be the new leader of The Woods. In light of that fact—"

"Excuse me," said Wing, interrupting, "Owl does not have the power to select any animal to be the new leader. We have elections to do that."

"Alright, alright," said Sniff. "Owl *nominated* me to be the new leader. That's not my point. My point is that I will make my last exhibition run of the season—free of charge to all—through The Hard Way at Owl's last Appearance. Owl himself, our great leader, has requested this exhibition run, so I will be happy to comply. In fact—and this is a fact with teeth—I intend to break my record by running *under* one minute!" There was more applause now; Sniff raised the microphone a moment, and smiled. "This run, I can promise you," he said, "will be a super-record run, which all of you will be able to witness together."

The applause continued, there was stamping and yelling and clapping by all of the rats, and many of the other four-footed animals. When the noise died down, Wing spoke up: "That should be a breathtaking—I mean, *really* breathtaking—run. I can't wait to be a witness."

There was more applause—some for Wing but most for Sniff. "Thank you, thank you, thank you," said Sniff, and then, lowering his microphone until the noise subsided, he raised it again and went on: "Now listen up, all of you. According to Owl, and based on the election rules, any animal who wants to be a candidate for leader of The Woods must declare officially by this coming Monday, at the Oak, no later than eight a.m. The same week, on Friday, of course, at six p.m., according to the rules, we'll have Owl's last Appearance, followed by the election. Now since I'm a candidate for leader, it will only be fair if Number Two takes my place up here on The Big Limb, to conduct the election."

"Wait a minute—is that fair?" said Wing. "I mean, having a deputy of yours up there in your place? How about having a deputy-rat alongside *another* animal, not of your own kind, to give the proceedings some fairness and balance?"

"Well now," said Sniff. "Do you have anyone in mind for the job?"

"Yeah I do," said Wing. "How about me?"

"You?" said Sniff, sniffing, seeming to be caught off guard, searching for words.

"Yes. Me," said Wing, turning to the crowd: "How does that sound to the others here—doesn't it make sense what I'm asking for?"

There was some applause and cheering, especially among the birds and squirrels.

"You mean," said Sniff, "two masters of ceremony on The Big Limb? Number Two, the greatest announcer in the history of The Woods, and a hawk-po-et?" He smiled and sniffed.

"Fair enough?" said Wing, looking at the crowd, and waving a wing.

Many applauded.

"Okay," said Sniff. "It's a deal, and in fact, I'll go further—after all, I've always been known for my fairness—I'll make sure there's another microphone, just for you—now isn't that a generous act on my part?" Sniff looked down and smiled at the applauding audience. "Okay. That's settled," he said. "Now here's how the proceedings will go. After my record exhibition run, we'll have the voting. The candidate who gets the most ayes will be our new leader."

There was more applause, and when it settled down, Sniff went on: "And now, let me address another terribly important concern. This is a concern of huge importance, of moral importance."

"Now we're gonna have a lecture on morality?" said Wing.

"This is a matter that has to do not only with today," said Sniff, "but with tomorrow and the next day, and the next week, and next year and beyond. This is a matter, Animals of The Woods, that has to do with survival itself—yours, mine, the survival of all of us, the survival of—"

"Come on," said Wing, "get to your point."

"I am talking about survival itself," said Sniff. "Whether we are to continue living as a community depends on how we deal with this great matter."

"Hurry up and tell us more," said Wing, "our curiosity is on fire and you're fanning the rising flames."

"Animals of the Woods," said Sniff, "we must destroy Fox before he destroys us!"

Now fear was alive in the crowd. The animals looked around at one another. They *felt* the fear; hair and fur stood up; eyes, as well as mouths, opened wide; many gasped for air and felt a tightness in their throats, and their groins. Sniff went on: "I repeat—in order for The Woods to survive, Fox must be destroyed." Sniff raised a paw over his head and gazed gravely down at the stricken faces, and continued: "There have been reports that Fox's killings have increased to a substantial level. Just in the last two days, fourteen bodies were found, horribly mutilated, and bleeding. Ten raccoons, three chipmunks, and one skunk. And this, Animals of The Woods, was not the act of a mere predator. It was the brutal act of an *assassin*."

"An assassin, really?" said Wing.

"An assassin, no less," said Sniff, "and that, animals of The Woods, is definitely a fact with teeth. This was the horrible deed of an animal that kills simply for the joy of killing. This is an animal that kills because he wants to destroy all of us. And let me tell you, Animals of The Woods: Fox will not stop until he has accomplished his bloody and brutal mission. He will not stop until—he will not stop until, and unless—"

"Until and unless what?" said Wing to the hushed and attentive crowd.

"Until and unless we stop him," said Sniff. "And listen: until we decide that we have had enough, and until we as a community, combining all of our resources—all of our brains and all of our claws and all of our teeth—and kill this awful killer!"

Now the applause was deafening. Sniff stood up straight, squared his shoulders, waving a paw over the heads below him, over the wild applause that lasted for nearly twenty seconds.

"Animals of the Woods," Sniff continued, "listen to my words, because words speak just as loud as actions . . . the only question is not *whether* Fox needs to be destroyed, but *how* and *when* Fox will be destroyed." Sniff paused again, and let the noise rise for a moment more, then raised a paw again, calmed the crowd once more, and continued: "We all know that all great things are first dreamed, and then realized. I must remind you that The Maze—that wonderful community project, which is providing all of us with a mental as well as a physical challenge, and which is a most fitting way of carrying on The Great Tradition established by Owl—was at first a dream of mine. But I want to tell you about another, more recent dream of mine, which is about to be realized. My dream this time was about a new machine, a marvelous machine. With this machine, my fellow animals of The Woods, we can solve our problem with Fox. And not only that. With this modern machine, which, by the way, will be expensive to design and to build and to operate—with this machine we can solve all of our other problems too."

"And what would these 'other problems' be?" said Wing.

"With this machine," said Sniff, waving off the question, "we can solve *all* of the problems of The Woods. In fact, with this machine, we can kill hundreds of birds with one acorn."

"Funny, funny," said Wing.

"I thought you'd like that," said Sniff, looking at Wing and smiling. "But seriously, with this machine, we can realize a peaceful and happy life, forever."

"This must be quite a machine," said Wing, cocking his head.

"Not only is this quite a machine," said Sniff. "This may be the greatest machine in the history of The Woods."

"Tell us more about your wonderful Dream Machine," said Wing. "We're dying for details."

"This is a machine that will enable us to make life in The Woods not only great but perfect," said Sniff.

"Really?" said Wing.

"Yes," answered Sniff. "I cannot at this point in time tell you when the Great Machine will be completed. I cannot at this point in time tell you what the Great Machine will look like, exactly. But I can tell you this. If we start immediately to raise money toward the realization of this, my fortunate Dream, we can one day, not far off, have our Dream Machine."

"Money, money, money!" shouted Wing. "Here we go again."

"Animals of The Woods," said Sniff, "we are getting closer and closer to realizing The Dream. And when The Dream is realized, when the Great Machine is finished, it will allow us to put an end to the violent and bloody destruction that Fox is causing in The Woods. And here is the truly wonderful thing about this invention, Animals of The Woods."

"Hurry up, tell us," said Wing.

"The truly wonderful thing about the Great Machine is that it will take only the simple pushing of keys on a keyboard to destroy Fox and to change The Woods into a perfect kingdom for all of us, forever."

"That *is* wonderful," said Wing. "Yeah, *really* wonderful!"

"Yes, it *is* wonderful," said Sniff. "And let me say this: only a true leader will be able to operate such an important machine."

"You mean the one who wins the upcoming election?" said Wing.

"Only he could do it," said Sniff. "I'm so glad you made my point for me. Only the winner of the election, who must be a leader, and it wouldn't hurt if that leader was the champion maze runner of The Woods. That for sure is a fact with teeth."

"*Gnawing* teeth, you mean?" said Wing. "A fact with *gnawing* teeth."

Sniff ignored Wing and went on: "But with all of our efforts, and with plenty of money from our Dream Machine Fund, which will be inaugurated today, very soon we will have our machine, and very soon this machine will be working for us to change The Woods to a perfect place, the New Woods, instead of the Old Woods. After all, the Old Woods, I must tell you, is finished, dead."

"You mean *are* finished," said Wing. "*Woods* is a plural word."

"Okay, the Old Woods *are* finished," said Sniff, "and thanks to our resident po-et and his vast vocabulary."

Sniff paused, let the animals take it all in, and repeated: "The Old Woods Are Dead. Death to the Old Woods!"

"Death to the Old Woods!" echoed The Five, and many others echoed the chant: "Death to the Old Woods! Death to the Old Woods! Death to the Old Woods!"

Then most in the crowd took up the chant: "Death to the Old Woods! Death to the Old Woods!" When the shouting diminished, Sniff continued: "But let me tell you, Animals of The Woods. The Old Woods is—I mean The Old Woods *are*—no longer useful. From now on, in the New Woods—after we get our new leader and our Great Machine—life will be different. No longer, as in the Old Woods, will life be chaotic. In the New Woods, there will be order, a new system of living, and only those who fit in will survive. I tell you, Animals of the Woods, the day of realization is quickly approaching. The Great Machine will soon save us from destruction, and create the happy life, that is, what I call The Kingdom of Sharing. And in The Kingdom of Sharing, he who is unfit will not survive. He who cannot cooperate will not find a home. We the survivors, the chosen, will walk over the empty eye sockets and the broken and decayed bones of the unfit, the lost. FOREVER!"

That did it. Most of the ground animals—led by The Five, who were now yelling and baring their teeth—were ecstatic, wild, insane with applause, and leaping into the air and yelling and stamping their feet.

When the noise and chaos finally subsided, Sniff raised a paw. "And now, Animals of the Woods," he said, "it is time for sharing, it is time to realize The Kingdom of Sharing." At the word *sharing* The Five began to stand at attention.

"I'm sure many, if not all of you," said Sniff, "have heard the story of my fight with Fox. That day he attacked me at the edge of The Woods, I fought him with everything I had, all my strength and courage. And why did I fight Fox?"

"To save yourself!" shouted Wing.

"I fought Fox for one reason," said Sniff. "I fought him for the sake of The Woods, for all of *you*. I fought Fox to save The Woods. It was not a personal dual, it was for you (pointing down at some individuals) *you*, and *you*, and *you,* and *you.* It was for all of you." The crowd kept applauding and roaring approval.

"And now you must be witnesses to the result of that violent fight: look at my left ear," he said, turning his head to the crowd to display his ear. There was a very small nick in it, barely noticeable, and too far away from the crowd for any animal to see it. "And now, each one of you—all of you—must share my struggle."

The Five had their next cue: they began to move about in the crowd, pointing down at fallen leaves at the feet of the animals, at times picking up a leaf and giving it away.

"Listen," said Sniff. "All of you, my fellow animals, take up a leaf, or accept one from The Five. Then hold the leaf. Cherish the leaf."

Sniff paused, looked down serenely at his feet, closed his eyes until there had been enough time for all of the animals to pick up a leaf—or to accept one offered by one of The Five. Then The Five returned to their place in front, each clutching a leaf, conspicuously.

"Now I want you to hold this leaf," Sniff said, opening one eye, "and when I say *eat*, take a bite from the leaf. This means that you are sharing my struggle with Fox, you are eating my agony, my struggle—with Fox." He paused again. *"Now—eat."*

All of the ground animals began to nibble on the leaves.

"And now, remember," Sniff said: "at this sacred moment in time, we are all sharing; we are all one in The Kingdom of Sharing."

The animals were absolutely calm. They stood with their heads bowed—quiet, attentive, captivated, as if renewed, until Sniff said, "Thank you, thank you." All of the animals opened their eyes, as The Five, moving among them with their cups, took up the first collection for the Dream Machine Fund.

When the collection was finished, the Appearance ended. Quietly. Reverently.

22: What Is a Sniff?

Early the next morning, Sniff and Number Two were standing on The Big Limb, just as, a few hundred rabbit hops away, Wing and Butterfly were perched on a limb of an ash tree. Number Two was broadcasting his sayings to The Woods in his soaring voice:

DEATH TO THE OLD WOODS!
LIFE TO THE NEW WOODS!
DEATH TO THE OLD WOODS!
LIFE TO THE NEW WOODS!

THE KINGDOM OF SHARING
IS THE KINGDOM OF CARING!
THE KINGDOM OF SHARING
IS THE KINGDOM OF CARING!

TEETH FOR LEADERS!
WINGS FOR CHEATERS!
TEETH FOR LEADERS!
WINGS FOR CHEATERS!

UP, UP AND AWAY
NEVER SAVES THE DAY!
UP, UP AND AWAY
NEVER SAVES THE DAY!

After a brief pause, Number Two announced his second group of sayings:

LEADERS TAKE THE HARD WAY!
LEADERS TAKE THE HARD WAY!

OLD WOODS DEAD, NEW WOODS AHEAD!
OLD WOODS DEAD, NEW WOODS AHEAD!

DO A GOOD DEED TODAY—OR ELSE!
DO A GOOD DEED TODAY—OR ELSE!

After another customary pause, it was Sniff's turn to take the microphone:

"WEEEEEEEEEEEEEEEEEEEE!" he shouted in his shrill voice.

From far away came Wing's response, "IIIIIIIIIIIIIIIIIIIII!" making Butterfly's wings tremble.

There was one more "WEEEEEEEEEEEEEEE!"

And one more "IIIIIIIIIIIIIII!"

Then all was quiet.

"Now that you've heard all of the announcements of the day," Wing said to Butterfly, "would you like to hear my new catalog essay, which I'm calling, 'What Is a Sniff?'"

"I would love to hear it," said Butterfly, relaxing by opening and closing her wings. She knew that Wing committed all of his writings to memory.

"It may be a little rough yet," said Wing, "but it goes like this:

'*A Sniff is a synonym for liar*

A Sniff is a synonym for cheater

A Sniff is a synonym for bully

A Sniff assumes he is superior to any other animal and therefore should be in charge of The Woods

A Sniff never feels shame

A Sniff never has regrets

A Sniff can never feel embarrassed or humiliated

A Sniff assumes that the meaning of The Woods is money

A Sniff has empathy only for his kind

A Sniff assumes that he is always right and therefore never wrong

A Sniff assumes that your business is his business

A Sniff doesn't accept facts or evidence if they don't support his opinions or feelings

A Sniff can tell sixty lies inside sixty seconds

A Sniff can make whatever he does or thinks—however meager or trivial—seem at least a hundred times more important than it actually is

A Sniff needs to be always celebrating his successes, all of which are self-concocted

A Sniff lacks curiosity, unless money is involved, or asserting power over others

A Sniff can take credit for the good deeds and ideas of others, without seeming to take credit for them

A Sniff will do anything to get what he wants: cheat, lie, steal, mislead, forge, deceive, trick, stiff, delude, con, beguile, dupe, defraud, betray, hoodwink, embarrass, humiliate, excoriate, misrepresent, falsify, defraud, wheedle, swindle, sweet talk, mystify, confuse, flatter, beg, bribe, obfuscate, cajole, obliterate, maim, do away with, etc.

A Sniff can pat you on the back with one paw and pick your pocket with another one

A Sniff insists that words speak louder than actions

A Sniff might as well be a separate species: Rattus audacitatus, or Rattus obliteraticus, because his main goal is to destroy those animals who are unrelated to him—or whose opinions and living habits differ from his own—'" Wing stopped.

"Is that the full essay?" asked Butterfly.

"No, that's not the half of it," said Wing. "But it's enough for now; I don't want to bore you with my extended catalog."

"You haven't bored me," said Butterfly. "I like it. It's excellently written and I think it's mostly true."

"Thank you," said Wing. "'Mostly true,' you say?"

"Your essay makes me wonder about something you said recently," said Butterfly.

"And what was that?" said Wing.

"I remember you saying that quite often you've noticed that whenever you turn your attention to one or the other side of an argument," said Butterfly, "you can see both sides as being convincing."

"So what does that have to do with my essay?" said Wing.

"Well," said Butterfly, "don't you think there might be at least one single thing about Sniff that's not one hundred percent negative?"

"I'll admit it," said Wing. "My essay is very one-sided. But I think you'll agree that, when you are in a war, it's so easy to assume that your enemy is totally evil—and that you yourself are totally good."

"Yes, I think that's true," said Butterfly, who became silent for a moment, then changed the subject: "Here's another question for you," she said. "If not Sniff as the leader, then who?"

"I'm glad you asked that question," said Wing. "I've given that some thought too, and I lean toward my friend, Claws. I think he'd make a fine leader."

"Just now," said Butterfly, "when you mentioned Claws it occurred to me, from what I've heard about him, that he and Sniff don't have very many characteristics in common."

"That's for sure," said Wing. "Of course, one thing they *do* have in common is their competitiveness. I know Claws well, and I can vouch for his honesty, his empathy, his imagination, and sense of fairness, as well as his strong sense of excellence. I'd say he's as genuine as they come. And here's another thing about him that I can vouch for."

"And what is that?" said Butterfly.

"Let me tell you, with his exact words, what he said to me recently," said Wing. "He said he has what he called 'a double life—one is on the ground, the other is in trees.' That's it! Claws is able to span at least two realms of life—the one with us winged creatures, and the other one, on the ground, with ground animals. That's an admirable quality in a leader, don't you think?"

"Yes, I would say so, for sure," said Butterfly.

"I'll definitely be encouraging him to run for leader," said Wing, "and I hope you'll join me."

"It goes without saying," said Butterfly.

"Then let's also hope," said Wing, "that a whole lot of non-Sniffians show up for the election. I'd like to see at least a plague of doves."

"And a horde of crows?" said Butterfly.

"And a scurry of squirrels?" said Wing.

"And maybe even a kaleidoscope of butterflies?" said Butterfly, her wings fluttering.

"That would be dazzling!" said Wing. Then the two said goodbye and flew away, both of them eager to hear from the brain expert, The Crow.

23: Delayed Response

Claws knew that the short poem he'd written, and hung up near his nest for others to see—especially Sniff—was sincere and clear, even if it had only three lines. But he was thinking that his response to Sniff had not been forceful enough. And also, he felt that he should've been able to think of the words at the exact moment Sniff told him that he no longer had a home in The Oak (as if he, Sniff, could be the sole owner of the great tree!). In truth, who would read Claws' poem (which was, to Claws, more of a sign-poem than a real poem anyway), way up in the highest branches of a tree? Not Sniff, certainly; he never had any reason to be climbing higher than The Big Limb.

So Claws decided to locate his friend, Wing, the best poet of The Woods, and have a talk, if possible. If Wing didn't know how to use words and use them with force, then nobody did.

"Before I show you a poem," said Claws, sitting on a cottonwood branch with Wing, "can I ask you a question?"

"Sure," said Wing.

"What if I write a poem," said Claws, "and it happens to be a way of getting back at another animal—sort of like getting even? Is that okay?"

"Can I guess what animal you're talking about?" said Wing.

"Sniff," said Claws. "He told me he's already the leader of The Woods, and that he's the owner of The Oak, so I can't live there anymore. Can you believe it?"

"I can believe it," said Wing. "There's all kinds of reasons for making poems or stories. I wouldn't worry about the reason you make a poem. I'd worry a lot more about the poem itself. Does it work, do all the parts come together, and speak to each other well? Are the words the best you can come up with to say what you want to say? The poem or story, whatever the reason for its origin, will always have its own life—in a sense, unconnected with why it was created."

"Okay," said Claws. "That makes some sense." He handed a poem to Wing, who began to read the first several lines, then said: "The main problem here is that the poem is rime-directed."

"Rime-directed? What does that mean?" said Claws.

"It means that the rimes are not natural, and the only way for rimes to work well in a poem is for them to be natural, or appropriate to what the poem is saying. The rimes have to come according to the setting of the poem, along with everything else in it: the images, the sounds, the figurative language, and so on."

"Can you be more specific?" said Claws.

"Right here, now," said Wing, holding up Claws' poem and pointing to the opening lines: "When you say, 'Consider the lowly rat, wearing his ugly hat,' the problem is that, even though 'rat' and 'hat' rime, the truth is that the second line is rime-directed. Its only reason for existing is to match the word 'rat' in the first line. In other words, it's a *forced* rime, that is, it's rime directed."

"Well, how could I improve it?" asked Claws.

"Why not just drop that second line and see what else can go with the first line, which I think is pretty good. I mean, it's true: rats *are* lowly animals—at least some are lowly, maybe a lot of them."

"You like that line?" said Claws.

"Sure," said Wing, "but I'm not just talking about my personal opinion of rats, I'm talking about the poem *as a poem*. We both agree on the first line's general truth, but just because a line is truthful doesn't necessarily mean it's a good line of poetry."

"But I thought poems had to be truthful," said Claws.

"They do," said Wing, "but that word 'truthful' is hard to define—whether it means something *inside* a poem or something *outside* of it. It's deceptive. Truth *outside* a poem is not the same as truth *inside* a poem. Well, it is, in a way; but what's most important is truthfulness *inside* a poem, which may or may not correspond exactly with truthfulness *outside* a poem, in The Woods."

"I don't quite understand that," said Claws. "Can you say it another way for me?"

"I mean that a poem has to stand on its own," said Wing. "It creates its own world—an inside world that's different from the outside world, and yet is based on the outside world. Does that make any sense?"

"No," said Claws, "I can't catch your meaning, I'm afraid."

"Okay. Let me put it this way," said Wing (realizing that what he'd just told Claws didn't make a lot of sense to himself either—he had a point to make but wasn't sure, at least right then, what exactly it was and how to make it. Yet he had to go on saying *something*—Claws expected him to know what he was talking about). "You have to be just as interested in words themselves—what they sound like, what they feel like when you say them or hear them, how they mix with other words—in order to make good poems. At one level, at least, words are just words and nothing else."

"Okay," said Claws. "Say I am really interested in words, which I am. Then what must I do to get better as a poet?"

Wing paused, then continued. "Make a lot of poems, read a lot of poems, observe animals, including yourself— how you all live, where you all live and so on—and never quit making poems, and reading a lot of them, and never quit observing. And, for sure, cherish your curiosity."

"That's it?" said Claws.

"That's pretty much it," said Wing. "But I'll add two more things."

"Two more things?" said Claws.

"First," said Wing, "trust yourself. Write about what *you* know and what *you* feel and what *you* think, and don't let anybody else tell you how to do it—not me, not anybody. Does that make any sense?"

"I think so," said Claws. "In other words, nobody else can make my poems. Right?"

"Exactly," said Wing.

"And I should appreciate that fact a lot, right?" Claws said.

"Right," said Wing. "A whole lot."

"And you had one more thing to add?" said Claws.

"Yes," said Wing. "But this is a little to the side of our discussion. You mentioned Sniff earlier, that he told you that he owns the tree you have your home in."

"Yes, that's true," said Claws.

"Well," said Wing. "Nobody, including Sniff, has the right to your home, your place in The Woods. Have you ever thought of challenging Sniff for the leader of The Woods?"

"Yes, I have," said Claws. "And others have also said I should become a candidate for leader. But do you think I'd have a chance?"

"I do," said Wing. "Consider this: you'd make a good leader, if only for the reason that you're an animal that lives both on the ground and in the air. You know about both worlds, as you recently told me, with elegance and power. And Sniff, being a ground animal, knows only about one world. It's a very narrow viewpoint compared to your much more comprehensive viewpoint."

"I hadn't thought of that," said Claws.

"Anyway," said Wing, "I hope you'll go for it, because I think you can win, and if you do, The Woods will be a lot better off as a result."

"Thank you," said Claws, "I appreciate your confidence in me. What do I owe you for your professional advice?"

"Nothing," said Wing. "We're friends."

Claws then thanked Wing for the good conversation, and Wing said he'd be glad to see more poems sometime if Claws would like to show them to him, and then he flew away.

That night, as Claws lay in his nest—a deep bowl of darkness—getting drowsier and drowsier, he made two decisions: first, that he would definitely become a candidate for the leader of The Woods. And second, that his short poem, attached to a branch near the top of The Oak, was nothing less than a delayed response to Sniff, which was better than no response at all. Of course, he knew that there were other issues to consider: that Sniff would probably never see his poem; and that he had a habit of making fun of poetry anyway.

And yet, and yet: a delayed response to Sniff was better than no response at all. It *was* better. It *was*, he kept saying to himself until he fell asleep.

24: Temptation

One of the latest rumors in The Woods was the weight gain of Spider. Lately, with a total of her main web and twelve dead-end webs—and having consumed four courting males, even in the last two days—she was beginning to feel the fine mesh of her main web giving more and more under her fat feet, even when freshly repaired.

So, she decided to go to The Maze and have a talk with Number Three. Although she had been visiting her webs daily, she hadn't done a single maze-run since the building of The Maze. But she had been thinking that maze-running itself might be a good way to lose weight.

"Would you put me on a maze-running exercise program?" she asked Number Three.

"Sure," said Number Three. "How many times a week could you come here to exercise?" (Spider had permission from Sniff to use The Maze anytime she wanted, free of charge.)

"Well, how about every day?" said Spider. "I'm already spending some time here, checking my webs." Number Three knew what she meant with her words, "checking my webs."

"Okay," he said to her, "but can I make a suggestion?"

"What's that?" said Spider.

"I don't think it's a good idea to do two things at once," said Number Three.

"Two things at once?" asked Spider.

"Yes," said Number Three. "What I mean is that it wouldn't be a good idea to come here to exercise, and then also to eat bugs."

"What difference does it make?" said Spider.

"I just think it's better to do one thing at a time," said Number Three. "That way, you'll be able to concentrate better."

"Okay, when can I start my program?" asked Spider.

"Right now, if you want to," said Number Three.

"I'm ready," Spider said.

"Okay," said Number Three, who accompanied Spider to the Easy Beginning. "Now for this first run-through, why don't you just concentrate on going at a slow, steady pace, and think only about The Way—which you yourself designed, don't forget—and nothing else. Just focus on direction and turns. Okay?" Spider was happy to hear the good words about her professional work.

"Sure," she said, and scuttled inside. About ten minutes later she came back around to The Beginning. She was puffing hard.

"How did it go?" asked Number Three.

"There's just one problem," said Spider.

"What's that?"

"Temptation."

"Ah yes, I see," said Number Three. "It takes a little time, this maze running." He handed Spider his booklet entitled 'Goals and Techniques of Maze Running.' "Not only do I talk about goals here (pointing at the booklet), but there's also pictures of techniques you need to learn and practice. The book is free for you, of course. Tomorrow we'll have another workout. Same time?"

"Yes, same time," said Spider. "That's great, I'm excited."

The next day Spider was back at The Maze, looking renewed and spirited.

"Did you read the chapter on goals?" asked Number Three.

"I sure did."

"And so, you have a goal now, is that right?"

"Yes, I've got my goal."

"Which is?"

"Can we keep this confidential?"

"Sure, it's all in confidence."

"My goal is to lose weight."

"Good," said Number Three. "Now, as you go through, I want you to have only your goal in your mind, and nothing else. Not techniques, not anything but your goal."

"Yes!" shouted Spider, and she scuttled through the entrance. About ten minutes later she came back, puffing hard again.

"Well? Good run?" asked Number Three.

"No," said Spider, looking downcast.

"Temptation?"

"Temptation."

"Okay," said Number Three. "Now I want you to go home and read the second chapter, on techniques, and have a good look at the material on nose-tailing. And tomorrow when you come back, we'll see what we can do about those temptations of yours. When one thing won't work, we try another. Right?"

"I'll try it," said Spider, who did have some patience left.

The next day Spider was again looking spirited and renewed, ready to begin over, ready to shed some weight.

"This time, when you go through," said Number Three, "I want you to think only about techniques, maze techniques. Did you read that chapter?"

"Yes, I read it twice," said Spider.

"And how about the material on nose-tailing?" he asked.

"I liked it," said Spider, "but I don't have a tail like you and the other four-legged animals."

"That's okay," said Number Three. "Just pretend that you have one. The nose tail is a mental concept anyway."

"No, I understand the technique thoroughly," said Spider, and burst through the entrance. Ten minutes later she came back around, puffing hard, looking downcast again.

"Temptation?" said Number Three.

"Temptation," said Spider.

"Again?"

"I just can't help it."

"You need to work on technique, and it takes a little while to get it down," said Number Three. "After that, it should be easy."

"No, it's not working," said Spider. "Every time I pass a web, I just have to check it. And then when I check it and there's a bug in it, I have to sting it and eat it. I can't help it," she said.

"Okay, here's another idea that may help," said Number Three.

"Tell me," said Spider, who was looking desperate and still breathing hard.

"Think about what you're doing inside The Maze," said Number Three. "Use your reasoning powers. Consider the fact that you have to burn up more energy and eat less. Just keep that foremost in your mind. It's like a formula: more energy output, less bug intake. You and I both know that the only way you can lose weight is to burn up more energy. That's why you're here, isn't it? Isn't that what your goal is? To shed some weight?"

"That's my goal," said Spider. "But something inside me is telling me something else."

"Telling you what?" said Number Three.

"Something inside me is telling me that my real goal is to eat as many bugs as possible," said Spider.

"Temptation, huh?"

"Temptation."

"Well, what can I say?" said Number Three, who hated to say those words but couldn't help saying them. "I want to help you achieve your goal."

"I know, but maybe I shouldn't come here at all," said Spider.

"Why not?"

"Because all I'll do is eat more bugs."

"Maybe that should be your new goal."

"My new goal?"

"Sure. To lose weight by staying away from The Maze."

"What a brilliant idea. I think I'll give it a try."

"Good," said Number Three, "but come back sometime and visit us anyway." He meant it. It was a warm farewell. And Spider said she would, of course, come back some time to visit, and said goodbye, and left.

And she did come back, the very next day.

"I thought about the conversation we had yesterday," Spider said.

"And what did you decide?" asked Number Three.

"Here's what I finally decided," she said. "I decided that when you have bugs in your webs, why not eat them, and get some exercise on the way to and from the webs?"

"Why not?" said Number Three, and both of them had a little laugh, after which Spider, once again, scuttled into The Beginning.

25: First Therapy Session

Claws was steadily improving his times in his maze-runs. Even though he and Number Three were competitors, they had become good friends, sharing their knowledge of running techniques.

Just as Claws was approaching Sniff's so-called Easy Way record (he knew he'd never equal Number Three's unofficial records), he'd been motivated to take up the challenge of the new Hard Way. Breaking Sniff's Hard Way record (not knowing it had been set by running through a tunnel) would be, Claws realized, extremely difficult if not impossible, but, as he had told Sniff, he was no quitter. The squirrel tail, which Claws thought he had escaped in his move from The Easy Way, he was not happy to learn, had followed him to The Hard Way, even though The Five were still doing their morning runs in The Easy Way. Number Three had tried to convince Sniff that the tail was a distraction to some maze-runners, and ought to be eliminated, but Sniff had huffed off the request. Number Three knew that the reason had to do with Sniff's feelings about his main competitor, the animal with the real squirrel tail.

Claws had memorized many sentences in Number Three's instruction booklet, his favorite pair being: "Don't worry about your opponent's speed. Increase your own speed and his will decrease in comparison."

Yet even though Claws took those words seriously, he was still not satisfied with his improvement. And he was still sometimes struggling with his stubborn instinct of leaping upward during his runs, as well as experiencing the sensation of being tripped up, whenever he was having an exceptionally good run.

"As far as the tripping goes," Number Three (who knew about the tunnel and that Sniff no longer needed vigilantes) kept telling him, "I really think it's all in your head. Just keep at it, keep running" was Number Three's advice. "You'll be improving your time. You know that the breakthroughs, with anything—writing poetry, running—come only with more and more work."

Claws appreciated Number Three's advice, but he still felt that he had to find a way to improve his concentration and, consequently, he assumed, his speed.

He'd heard that Number Four had recently become a licensed psychologist and was taking patients after work and on weekends. He disliked the idea of having to go to a psychologist for counseling, but he felt that he might learn something useful to him, as a maze-runner.

So, on Monday after work, Claws went to Number Four's office nest, which was only fifty or so rabbit hops from The Oak. A sign outside read: "Dr. Four, Psychologist, DSP"

Claws was greeted by a friendly-looking rat who, when he was on duty with The Five, could be somewhat cranky. "Well, good to see you, Claws," he said, in a calm voice. "Please come inside. What can I do for you?"

Claws stepped inside, "I'd like to talk to you about my maze-running," he said. "I've got a problem with my concentration and I was wondering if—"

"Certainly," said Dr. Four. "But before I accept a new client, he or she must meet two conditions."

"Conditions?" said Claws.

"Yes," said Dr. Four. "First, you must demonstrate a genuine desire to get better, or therapy cannot be effective. And second, the fee is seven dollars per session, to be paid upfront."

"Sounds alright to me," said Claws.

"Excellent," said Dr. Four, holding out a paw and smiling professionally.

"Oh, sure," said Claws, and he gave Dr. Four the money.

Dr. Four pointed to a soft bed of flattened-out grass on the floor. "Get down there, on your back," he said, "close your eyes, relax, pretend that you're floating on The Pond, and we can get started." Claws lay down and closed his eyes, trying to relax as best he could. Dr. Four then pushed a button on his alarm clock, took up a notebook and pencil, and touched the pencil to his tongue: "Well, now," he said, "I want to hear a little about your family life. Just relax, keep your eyes closed, and tell me about your background."

"My mother died last year," said Claws, "and my father died last year too. I've got two brothers and a sister."

"I see," said Dr. Four. "And what was your relationship with your father like, when he was alive?"

"I never saw him much; he was very busy," said Claws.

"I see," said Dr. Four. "And how about your mother—what was your relationship with your mother like?"

"It was good," said Claws.

"When you say it was good, does that mean the relationship between you and your father was not so good?" asked Dr. Four.

"No, I just knew my mother better," Claws said, "because I saw her more than I saw my father."

"Very interesting," said Dr. Four, and jotted some notes down. "Now tell me," he said, "what was your relationship with your siblings?"

"I got along with them fine," said Claws, "and I still do. We used to chase each other around and up and down trees mostly."

"Very interesting," said Dr. Four, jotting more notes down.

Claws opened one eye: "May I ask you," he said, "what my family has got to do with my concentration in The Maze?" (The words sounded a little too formal to Claws as he said them, but then he realized this was a formal situation.)

"Just keep your eyes closed, and relax," said Dr. Four. "Just answer my questions as I ask them; don't worry about anything else."

"Okay," said Claws, and he closed his eyes.

"Now tell me," said Dr. Four, "what was your father's occupation?"

"He was a mail carrier," said Claws.

"Very interesting," said Dr. Four. "And you've followed in his footsteps."

"Not really," said Claws.

"I thought you were also a mail carrier," said Dr. Four.

"Yes, I am, but I've got a different route," said Claws.

"I understand," said Dr. Four. "Now tell me this: did your father work out a lot, like you?"

"Yes, he liked to stay in shape for leaping contests."

"Leaping contests?" said Dr. Four.

"Yes," said Claws.

"You mean jumping contests?" said Dr. Four.

"No, I mean leaping," said Claws. "Jumping is what ground animals do. Leaping is what you do when you're up in the air, in the trees."

"Ah yes, I see," said Dr. Four. "Now tell me this, was he a better jumper than you?"

"You mean 'leaper'? I'd say we were pretty even," said Claws. "We both have the record."

"I see, very interesting," said Dr. Four. "And what record are you referring to?"

"From the ash to the elm," said Claws.

"Ah, yes," said Dr. Four. "It must be quite a jump—I mean, leap."

"It is," said Claws. "We're the only ones in the history of The Woods, as far as anybody knows, who made that leap."

"Most interesting," said Dr. Four. "But let me ask you this: Have you ever thought or dreamed of leaping even farther than your father?"

"I have thought about it," said Claws, "but I think more about being the fastest maze-runner."

Just as Dr. Four was making more notes, his alarm clock started buzzing.

"Time's up," he said, "but I do have one more question: What did your father die of?"

"He died leaping," said Claws.

"Really?" said Dr. Four. "Now that is very interesting."

"Yes, from the box elder to the ash," said Claws. "If he'd made it, it would've been even a greater leap than from the ash to the elm. But he missed it. My mother said he shouldn't've tried it because it was late in the year and he was heavier than when he leaped from the ash to the elm. But she said he was stubborn sometimes."

"That's most fascinating," said Dr. Four. "I'd like to explore this a little more the next time we meet."

"Okay," said Claws. Dr. Four made a note in his notebook, then went on: "But let me say here right now, even though the time is up—that it's quite clear to me that you will no doubt need to eventually come to terms with that great leap that your father didn't quite make."

"Really?" said Claws, opening his eyes and rubbing them.

"Yes, for sure," said Dr. Four. "And, that, I'm afraid, is the end of our first session. Goes fast, doesn't it?"

"It sure does," said Claws.

"Okay," said Dr. Four. "Next time we'll pursue your family background a bit more thoroughly, and then we can begin to address your maze-running problem. This first session was a good start."

"But can't you tell me anything about improving my concentration?" said Claws, who was now standing up on the matted grass.

"We'll come to that later," said Dr. Four, closing his notebook. "Therapy is an involved process. It takes time; it takes time."

"Oh," said Claws, rubbing his eyes again.

"Let's get together for at least one more session," said Dr. Four. "How about tomorrow, six p.m.?"

"I'll be here," said Claws, and he hurried away. When he was out of sight, Sniff walked in, quietly. He had been listening close by. "One more session ought to take care of this ambitious squirrel," he said.

"I agree, sir," said Number Four, and he gave six dollars to Sniff, who turned and walked away.

26: Claws Gets a Second Opinion

Early Tuesday morning, when Claws was at The Maze for his workout, he told Number Three about his meeting with Dr. Four. "He asked me a lot of questions about my family, but he didn't say anything about my problem with concentration."

"Have you ever heard of the story called 'The Wolf and the Happy Frog'?" asked Number Three.

"No," said Claws. "What's it about?"

"Once there was a wolf," said Number Three, "who hadn't been able to catch a rabbit for two weeks, so he was very hungry. He had heard of a frog in a nearby pond, who always seemed to be contented. The frog sat on a lily pad day after day, with his mouth wide open, and insects simply came along and flew into it.

"One day the wolf visited the frog. 'Tell me,' he said, 'what can I do to improve my hunting? I haven't caught a rabbit for two weeks and I'm terribly hungry.'

"'Here's what you need to do,' said the frog. 'Just go to the middle of a meadow and sit there, very still, with your mouth wide open. Eventually, a rabbit will come along and hop right into it.'

"'Thank you very much,' said the wolf, and he left. A short time later he began to sit, very still, in the middle of a meadow, with his mouth wide open, waiting for a rabbit to come by and hop inside. No rabbit came by, of course, because the ones who lived in the meadow could see or smell a predator from a distance, and so they avoided him.

"But the wolf persisted, all the while with a picture of the happy frog in his imagination. Three weeks later he died of starvation."

"And that's the story?" asked Claws.

"That's it," said Number Three. "And what do you think the moral is?"

"Patience doesn't always pay off?" said Claws.

"Wrong," said Number Three. "The wolf was foolish to go to a frog for advice about hunting."

"In other words," said Claws, "the wolf should've found another wolf and asked him. Is that right?"

"Wrong again," said Number Three.

"Why?" asked Claws.

"Think about it," said Number Three. "Why would one wolf give another wolf advice on how to hunt?"

Claws was silent for a long moment, thinking. "Okay," he said, "what you say does make some sense. But even if you and I are also different—you a rat and me a squirrel—at least whenever I ask you for advice about maze-running, I know I'm talking to the right animal."

"I like to think so," said Number Three, and the two friends had a good laugh together.

27: Yes Yes Yes

Claws had been wondering all day how Sniff could have the nerve to claim that he was the leader of The Woods, when Owl was still the actual leader. That was one thing he was wondering about, when he had a chance to rest a few minutes, on a limb. Other thoughts were chattering inside his furry head. One of them was that leaders like to compete, and to win, and if Sniff wouldn't accept his challenge to have a climbing or a leaping contest, he was looking forward to an even bigger competition: the election of the leader of The Woods! Especially since Sniff had called himself a leader and Claws a mere follower. "We'll see about that," he said aloud to himself.

Another thought in his head was: if he *did* become the leader of The Woods, would it be for a good reason? Would he be doing it mainly to get back at Sniff? Is that a good enough reason? Was it fair to the other animals, and to himself? Maybe it *was* fair. Or maybe it *wasn't*. Or maybe, if he thought like Frog, it was both fair and unfair at the same time.

Claws was improving his maze-time almost daily. Even though his instinct of leaping upward was diminishing, he was still troubled by the sensation of being tripped up, especially when he was having an exceptional run. "It's not *really* happening," he told Number Three that evening (and he was right, of course, since there were no vigilantes in The Hard Way), "but I still have a constant fear of it actually happening. So, I've decided that if the fear isn't going away, I might as well welcome it."

"You welcome the fear?" said Number Three.

"I welcome it, yes," said Claws. "And I want it to stay with me so much that I keep asking it to stay, I keep *begging* it to stay. Every time I make a run I keep saying to the fear, over and over, *yes yes yes*. And guess what? My maze-times are getting better and better *because of the fear*!"

"As I said before, Claws, it's all in your head," said Number Three.

28: Report from The Crow

Butterfly and Wing were talking deep inside a maple tree, which was gradually losing its leaves in cooler and cooler weather.

"So, The Crow only charged you five dollars—not bad," said Wing, giving Butterfly two and a half dollars. "How did your talk go?"

"Thank you, very well," said Butterfly. "I took a lot of notes during and afterward. Let me make sure I get this right (checking her notes). The Crow seems to have an impressive understanding of rat behavior, based on his brain studies, and he's been aware of Sniff for some time. He thinks Sniff is a special case. In fact, in his words—according to my notes here (reading)—Sniff is 'clearly an aberration.'"

"So, Sniff actually *has* a brain?" said Wing.

"Yes," said Butterfly. "The Crow says that Sniff's behavior suggests very strongly that he has a pronounced, or enlarged, A-Complex region at the back of his brain."

"A-Complex?" said Wing.

"Yes," said Butterfly "The A-Complex is that part of the brain that contains what's called the 'audacity factor.'"

"So, Sniff's got a lot of audacity—that's not exactly news, is it?" said Wing.

"Not at all," said Butterfly. "And not only that, but these same rats will also generally have what's called the 'Double-E-Complex.'"

"Double-E Complex? Scientists delight in their esoteric terminology, don't they?" said Wing.

"It seems so," said Butterfly. "The first E stands for empathy—which this kind of animal is lacking in—and the second E stands for a sense of entitlement, which this kind of animal has in great abundance."

"It all makes sense," said Wing. "And yet Sniff may not care for others, but that doesn't mean he doesn't care for himself, and his kin. And he's certainly not shy about claiming how entitled he is."

"That's true," said Butterfly.

"And did you bring up Sniff's so-called 'Kingdom of Sharing'?" said Wing.

"I did," said Butterfly, "and I forgot to mention that an enlarged A-Complex usually means the animal also has an enlarged capacity for deceit."

"And we already knew that Sniff may very well be the biggest deceiver in The Woods, didn't we?" said Wing.

"I agree," said Butterfly. "Actually, you reveal in your essay a lot of the things that The Crow said to me. For instance, he said that those animals with Sniff's brain structure refuse to play by the rules."

"That sounds like Sniff alright," said Wing.

"But then there's something else that The Crow told me about Sniff's brain that I thought was really interesting," said Butterfly.

"And what was that?" asked Wing.

"He said that if the A-Complex is in fact overly large," said Butterfly, "the characteristics of being very audacious and aggressive tend to cause an animal like this to slip up at times."

"Ah-ha," said Wing. "So, Sniff is mistake-prone? That's good information."

"And there's even more," said Butterfly. "The Crow said that this kind of animal possesses a huge 'fear factor.'"

"Fear?" said Wing. "I've seen the aggression and the audacity, but fear? Of what?"

"Snakes," said Butterfly.

"Snakes?" said Wing.

"That's right," said Butterfly.

"That, of course, explains the 'No Snakes' rule at The Maze," said Wing.

"I was thinking the same thing," said Butterfly.

"And so," said Wing, "this sniffing, metaphorical mutation of audacity, aggression, and fear also makes mistakes, and hates snakes. How about *that* for a line—'makes mistakes, and hates snakes'—four long-a sounds in the last five words in a row. Frog might say it's such a bad line that it's pure poetry."

"Makes mistakes, and hates snakes," said Butterfly. "It *is* sort of catchy."

"Thanks," said Wing. "but don't all rats hate snakes?"

"I asked The Crow about that," said Butterfly, "and he said it's true that all rats have a natural fear of snakes, especially rat snakes, but that some rats' fear, he said, is way beyond the norm. In fact, it can be as high as the

99.999999 percentile of fear—and he thought that Sniff might very well fit that description." Butterfly closed her notebook.

"Okay," said Wing. "Now, since we have our information from a true expert, why don't we use it?"

"What do you have in mind?" said Butterfly.

"Let's hire Snake to do away with our enemy, Sniff," said Wing.

"Never," said Butterfly, her wings suddenly shuddering. "If you're talking about murder. But if you mean hiring a snake to scare Sniff away, that's another matter."

"But maybe, realistically," said Wing, "doing away with Sniff is the only way we can stop him. Would we be wasting our time and money just scaring him?"

"The Law of The Woods says, very clearly in three words: 'No Unnecessary Killing,'" said Butterfly. "But there is no law that says we can't put such a scare into Sniff that he'd be forced to abandon his wicked ways."

"Of course Snake *is* a rat snake," said Wing.

"I know," said Butterfly.

"I know one thing for sure," said Wing. "He's got to be stopped, somehow. If he wins the election, we're all doomed, except for, of course, his own kind. But say a little more about why you think doing away with him is wrong."

"No Unnecessary Killing," said Butterfly. "It's the law; it's an absolute of The Woods. Without it, The Woods would be erased from existence, because any animal would have the license to do away with any other animal, just because they didn't like it."

"Or maybe because it would increase their status in The Woods," said Wing. Both of them paused, as if they'd run out of words. Wing shifted his weight slightly on the branch, then shrugged, and went on:

"Okay, I think you have a good argument. I can see going ahead and hiring Snake, if he'll agree to our terms. Since you had the conversation with The Crow, I can have a talk with Snake, if that works for you."

"That sounds good," said Butterfly,

"Maybe we can give Sniff a great big jolt of a scare," said Wing. "Big enough to start him off—at least we can hope—in a more benign direction. Maybe even, out of The Woods for good."

"I think that's our best strategy," said Butterfly.

And so, Wing and Butterfly flew away in their own direction, having agreed to have Wing locate Snake for a talk.

29: Second Therapy Session

For the second time, Claws was stretched out on Dr. Four's grassy office floor.

"Well now," said Dr. Four, "let's get started: are you aware of anyone in your family besides yourself who has an excessive fear of the ground?"

"I have an excessive fear of the ground? I didn't know that," said Claws.

"Yes," said Dr. Four. "You obviously hate being on the ground."

"I wouldn't say I hate it," said Claws.

"Is this fear of being on the ground," said Number Four, "something that you noticed, for example, in your father?"

"But did I actually tell you that I'm really scared to be on the ground?" said Claws.

"No, you didn't tell me directly," said Dr. Four, "but you gave me a strong hint of it in our last session together."

"But how did I do that?" asked Claws.

"You mentioned your father's great jump," said Dr. Four, "the one he didn't make—saying how much you'd like to try it yourself someday."

"Yes, I admire the leap my father tried to make," said Claws. "But if I said I wanted to try it myself, I didn't mean to. Actually, as I said before, I want to be the best maze-runner."

"Yes, well . . ." said Dr. Four, "you have a classic case of what is called in the profession, 'terraphobia,' which is an excessive fear of the ground."

"But I don't usually feel terribly scared just being on the ground," said Claws. "Well, maybe a little nervous, now that I think about it. But don't all squirrels have at least a little fear of being on the ground?"

"No," said Dr. Four. "You see, even if you don't *feel* scared, and even though you don't exhibit any outward symptoms of fear, you do agree, don't you, that you feel more comfortable when you're up in a tree, above the ground. Isn't that true?"

"That's true," said Claws.

"Alright, now that we've established your condition, let me again ask you: has anyone else in your family exhibited this same fear; that is, did your father feel more comfortable when he was in a tree than on the ground?"

"I don't know. I never asked him," said Claws.

"And your mother, how about your mother?"

"I never asked her either."

"And your siblings, how about them?"

"I never asked them either."

"You see," said Dr. Four, "not only are you terraphobic, but you also exhibit symptoms of what is called 'interrophobia.'"

"Interrophobia?"

"Yes," said Dr. Four. "As in 'interrogate,' asking questions. You have a fear of asking and/or answering questions."

"Such big words," said Claws.

"You will notice," said Dr. Four, "that both words, 'terraphobia' and 'interrophobia' have the same root, 'terre.' And of course the other same root, 'phobia,' which means fear."

"Yes," said Claws, "I know that a phobia means being scared of something."

"Back to the root, 'terre,'" said Dr. Four. "It means 'ground.' Have you ever heard the expression 'well-grounded'?"

"Sure," said Claws.

"'Well-grounded' means healthy," said Dr. Four. "Well-grounded animals are healthy because they have no fear of the ground and no fear of asking and/or answering questions."

"So, are you saying I'm not a well-grounded animal?" asked Claws.

"Yes, that may be part of your problem," said Dr. Four. "And if it's even a small part, then we need to know how far this problem goes back in your family tree—no pun intended—I mean, your family."

"But what difference does it make if others in my family have the same problem?" said Claws.

"Because once we can establish that the problem was inherited and not learned or acquired," said Dr. Four, "then we can begin to treat it effectively. Each origin requires a separate and special treatment."

"I see," said Claws.

"I want you to know," said Dr. Four, "that either problem, from either origin, is quite treatable. But if the origin is genetic, it's more difficult to deal with. I want to be honest with you, above all."

"But how can we find out?" asked Claws.

"Your father is the key," said Dr. Four.

"The key?"

"Yes," said Dr. Four, just as the alarm went off. "Time's up."

"Time's up?" said Claws, opening his eyes, and rubbing them.

"Yes, the session's over. Goes fast, doesn't it?"

"It sure does," said Claws. "But it's too bad we can't go on a little more on the subject of my father," said Claws.

"Well," said Dr. Four. "Just stay put for a moment, keep your eyes closed, and let me go on a little beyond my time. I won't charge you extra for this, and I do have another patient coming to see me shortly, but your case is especially interesting to me. In fact—and this is a fact with teeth—I have, I'll admit, found your case to be very interesting in these two sessions. So, let me go on and say one more thing that should be not only helpful to you, but probably life-saving."

"Oh, please do," said Claws.

"Let me say that, in order for you to become well-grounded, you must begin with the jump."

"The leap?" said Claws.

"Of course," said Dr. Four. "The leap."

"You mean I need to try to make the same leap my father tried, and missed?" said Claws. "The leap that killed him?"

"I'm afraid that that is exactly what I mean," said Dr. Four.

"I'll have to give that a lot of thought," said Claws.

"You really should," said Dr. Four, "because I believe it's the only way that your problem will be solved. The only way."

"The only way?" asked Claws.

"Yes," said Dr. Four, "the only way. And now I must close this session and get ready for my next patient."

Claws stood up. "Thank you," he said, and left, and going out the door he wondered why he had said *thank you* to Dr. Four, if he didn't actually mean it.

A moment later, Sniff stepped quietly inside. "Not bad," he said.

"Yeah, sir," said Number Four, then gave Sniff six dollars.

"I think we've got this politically ambitious squirrel right by the you-know-what," said Sniff.

"Acorns?" said Number Four.

"You got it," said Sniff. "This is one squirrel that is on his way down instead of on his way up." Sniff turned around and left.

30: To Leap or Not to Leap

For two straight hours after his meeting with Dr. Four, Claws had been sitting on the very same and very high branch of the box elder, from which his father had made his fatal leap.

He was staring at the perilous space between himself and the ash tree limb, a space that looked even more perilous because of the lack of leaves, from a recent frost. He looked at the branch which his father had tried to stab with his claws but instead stabbed air. Feeling some tension in his back legs, he was wondering, over and over, if he could plant his feet solidly on his takeoff branch, and spring into the air and snag that faraway branch. "Could I?" he asked himself over and over. And, over and over: "Should I?" he kept asking himself.

He thought, and thought, and thought, and thought— and thought.

Later that day, still thinking, and thinking, and feeling confused and tense, he happened to be climbing a tree and to come upon Butterfly, who was reading on a branch. Having heard Wing say that she was a student of such fields as philosophy and science, he asked her if the two of them could have a little conversation.

"Yes," she was happy to say, and Claws told her about his dilemma: how he had sat on the high branch of the box elder for a long time, how his leg muscles tensed up as he thought about springing into the air and leaping beyond his father to a great record, and how he simply couldn't make up his mind. "What do you think I should do?" he asked Butterfly.

"Have you ever considered the choice of not having to make a choice?" said Butterfly.

"Not having to make a choice?" said Claws.

"Yes," said Butterfly. "After all, is there a law that says you must make up your mind on this matter, or any matter, as long as not making up your mind doesn't hurt any animal in The Woods, including yourself?"

"I never thought of it that way," said Claws.

"In other words," said Butterfly, "let's say you have a variety of choices. You can say *yes* and take the leap, and miss and be hurt or killed—or you can choose to leap, and say you succeed, and set a great record your father failed at setting; or you can choose to say *no*, and not take the leap, and then perhaps regret it and fret about it for the rest of your life because you didn't try it. Or you can decide to make neither choice—to leap or not to leap. In other words, you can let go of the choices, and watch them fall, the way we're seeing leaves falling, right now, all over The Woods." Both of them looked out and down and watched some leaves falling all the way to the ground.

"I see," said Claws.

"But of course, it's up to you—it's your choice and only your choice that counts. Nobody else can choose for you," said Butterfly.

"Oh yes, I understand," said Claws. "I'll think it over. Thank you for your good ideas," he said, and left.

Claws went back to the box elder tree, climbed to the same, fateful, high limb again, and again sat there, looking out over the huge gap between the two trees. And once more, he thought, and thought, and thought. And thought. And thought. Once again, as he looked out and down, he felt something powerful stirring in his back legs, something that gave him a sudden rush of springiness, of confidence, but also agitation. He raised his back and braced himself for. . . *for what*? Then the tension and agitation, as well as the springiness, disappeared, and he relaxed, and climbed back down the tree.

That night as he lay in his nest, he decided to make the decision of not making the decision. Just as he was beginning to get drowsy, an uncomfortable feeling slipped into his mind, along with the thought that maybe not making up his mind on whether or not to leap was not really a decision at all, because it wasn't final enough—it didn't give him complete relief. He still felt there was something missing, something incomplete, about his so-called decision or non-decision. He didn't like the feeling, except that it contained the plain truth that he was still alive because he didn't try to make the leap, and then miss the claw-stab on the far branch. And besides, there didn't seem to be anything he could do about the feeling. And yet he began to realize that he could decide to just lie there in his nest, and accept what he was feeling—even, as in his maze runs, say *yes* to it—while at the same time yielding to the soft claws of sleep. Which finally happened.

31: Between Friends

Sniff was busy. Sniff was busy as a rat. He was Chair-rat or Head-Rat of many committees and groups, such as three ranking committees; The Charity Committee (CC); The Committee on Maze Rules (CMR); The Initiation of War Committee (IWC); The Prevention of War Committee (PWC); The Committee on the Abuse of Spearmint and Other Vices (CASOV); The Anti-Fox League (AFL); The Owl Retirement Fund (ORF); The Dream Committee (DC); The Committee on Population (CP); The Committee on Population Control (CPC); The Committee for a New Woods (CNW); The Body-Mind-Spirit Committee (BMSC); The Woods Ethics Committee (WEC); The Committee on Miscellaneous Matters (CMM); The Oak Restoration Fund (ORF) The Good Deed Society (GDS); The Slogan Committee (SC); The Committee Overseeing and Commanding All Other Committees (COCAOC), and most recently, the Dream Machine Fund, the Committee on the New Woods Election (CNWE), and The Committee on Exhibition Runs (CER).

Wing too was busy—busy hunting—but he had a little time to veer from his regular path and land on a cottonwood branch close to The Maze, and find a place where he couldn't be observed. Just then he heard "Go!" shouted by the starter, and watched a rat enter the Hard Way. Even though he had not before then been able to see into The Maze below him, because of the heavy canopy of leaves, on this day—not long after a frost—by moving his head quickly from side to side, he was able to get at least some glimpses of the maze-runner. He kept watching until the runner emerged from The End and heard the timer say, "two-forty-six!"

A moment later he heard a burst of applause from the small weekday audience and assumed that the noise had to be for Sniff, who was about to make his daily exhibition run. The starter shouted "Go!" and Sniff disappeared through the entrance. Wing waited, and kept watching, moving his head from side to side, focused (as he had with the first runner). For at least a minute he saw absolutely nothing moving. Then when he focused on The End, as with the first runner, he saw Sniff suddenly emerge, as if out of nowhere! The timer shouted, "one-twelve!" and the crowd noise rose again.

Wing immediately flew off to find Butterfly, who was perched on a familiar branch, making notes.

"Guess what I just saw?" he said.

"I've never been much of a guesser," said Butterfly.

"I just saw Sniff run through The Maze without running through The Maze."

"What? Say it again," said Butterfly.

"I said I just saw Sniff run through The Maze without running through The Maze," said Wing.

"That's very curious," said Butterfly. "How could that be?"

"I don't know for sure," said Wing, "but I've never been faulted for poor eyesight—I'm supposed to be awfully good at spotting small, four-footed creatures."

"Remarkable," said Butterfly. "Do you suppose—"

"Are you thinking what I'm thinking?" said Wing.

"That Sniff can make himself invisible?" asked Butterfly.

"No," said Wing. "That he's got a tunnel under The Maze—a shortcut."

"Well now," said Butterfly, "that would certainly explain why The Maze was closed for repairs last week, wouldn't it?"

"And also explain," said Wing, "why his so-called record times in his so-called Hard Way have been so fast—oh yes, and by the way, I just remembered another reason for the tunnel."

"What's that?" said Butterfly.

"Everybody knows that, just before The Maze was closed for so-called repairs, Claws was coming very close to Sniff's record. The one thing that Sniff can't stand is not being first, in anything. And now, he's finally got his easy way through the Hard Way. Another thing you can't fault Sniff for is lack of cleverness."

"And maybe also, determination," said Butterfly. "But a tunnel makes him King of The Maze, and therefore, in his mind, King of The Woods, paws down."

"Yes," said Wing, "but it looks like the tunnel could turn out to be one of those mistakes that The Crow spoke of in his analysis of Sniff's brain. He *did* say he's mistake-prone."

"Makes mistakes, and hates snakes?" said Butterfly.

"Ah-ha," said Wing, "you remembered."

"I did," said Butterfly.

"And another mistake has been his bad treatment of Claws," said Wing, "who also hates to come in second. This makes me feel almost certain that Claws is now officially a candidate for leader."

"Oh," said Butterfly, "I so much hope so."

"Now," said Wing, "shall we get going on that scenario we talked about—the one involving Snake and Sniff? 'Snake and Sniff'—notice how that s-n sound at the beginning of a word indicates something sort of creepy?"

"Yes, it does," said Butterfly. "'Snide, snoopy, snicker, snooty, snotty'—you're right. And yes, as to our agreed-on scenario. I'm beginning to see it clearly. How about something like this: Snake is hiding inside the tunnel, facing the entrance, and when Sniff comes through and gets a glimpse of him, he's stopped in his tracks, turns around and bolts back and out the entrance . . . or, if Sniff happens to get closer to Snake without seeing him, and Snake suddenly unhinges his jaw (as snakes seem to do), and Sniff gets a glimpse of that black maw, he turns around and flees. Then Snake follows after him, and slithers out of the entrance to the tunnel."

"For all to see," said Wing. "I like the vivid images you present, and especially that phrase, 'unhinges his jaw'—perfect!"

"Thanks," said Butterfly. "But I'm no poet."

"And our plan should work exceedingly well," said Wing, "since Sniff may have made his biggest mistake of all when he promised to break his own Hard Way record on that very day—and instead, he's stopped in his nefarious tracks."

"Inside his nefarious tunnel," said Butterfly.

"And I'm up there on The Big Limb," said Wing, "as one of the announcers—so I'm the animal with the job of explaining to the audience what's going on, and they will all be turned around and seeing the action for themselves, with their own eyeballs."

"Yes," said Butterfly.

"Okay," said Wing, "and all of the animals who show up for the election, even the Sniffians, will find out—in a very dramatic way—that Sniff is a fraud, a con-rat of the lowest kind."

"Let's get it done," said Butterfly.

"There's still some work ahead," said Wing, "but I believe we can make it all happen in our favor. First I've got to have a talk with a snake."

With those words, the two friends parted.

32: What If?

Sniff and Stub were talking under The Oak. "When do you think the Dream Machine will be built?" asked Stub.

"I don't know for sure," said Sniff, "but the sooner the better. We need to start making things happen around here."

"What's the first thing you'll do with the machine?" asked Stub.

"I'll have it installed in The Hole, under lock and key," said Sniff.

"And then what's the first action you'll take when the Dream Machine is plugged in and turned on?"

"I'll start getting rid of the creatures with wings, and the climbers," said Sniff. "Just by pushing the keys."

"How about Fox, then; what'll happen to Fox?" said Stub.

"I'll give him all kinds of grief," said Sniff.

"You'll get rid of him, won't you?" asked Stub.

"No, I won't exactly get rid of him."

"Why not? He's our biggest enemy in The Woods, isn't he?"

"He's a big one for sure, but he's the kind of enemy that you need to have around. The kind that gives the animals a purpose to live. You gotta have an enemy around all the time."

"But why have you been saying that you want to get rid of Fox?" said Stub.

"I say a lot of things," said Sniff, "and sometimes I mean what I say and sometimes I don't mean what I say. I could kill Fox if I wanted to, with the machine. But killing him by pushing a key or two would be too easy. And what reason to exist would the animals have without Fox out there threatening them?"

"But everybody's afraid of Fox. If he was out of the picture, there wouldn't be any more fear," said Stub, "or at least there'd be a lot less fear. I'm confused. I thought fear was bad."

"No, it's a good thing," said Sniff. "And I'll tell you something else, too, and this is another fact with teeth: I've already got my Dream Machine."

"You've already got it?" said Stub, with more wrinkles showing in his already-wrinkled countenance.

"Yes, I've got one, and it's working well. My Dream Machine is The Word."

"The Word?" said Stub.

"Yes, The Word," said Sniff. "All I have to do is say what I want done, and it'll get done. What counts, always, is who is using the words. That's all."

"I don't understand that," said Stub.

"I mean that it all depends on if the speaker is a leader, especially the one and only leader, or just a lowly follower," said Sniff. "If a leader is using the words, they count; if a follower is using them, they don't count. It's that simple."

"But aren't the words themselves important?" asked Stub. "I mean, doesn't it matter which words are being used?"

"No," said Sniff, "Not compared to who uses them. Look at the po-ets—they're all just followers, and so who cares what their po-ems say? But would you like an example of how my word machine works?"

"Yes, please give me an example," said Stub.

"Alright," said Sniff. "If I say on any morning to The Five: kill six birds apiece today and don't report back to me until you've got the six, then by evening, I'll have my thirty dead birds. See what I mean?"

"Yes, I see," said Stub. "So, if you said ten birds apiece, you'd get fifty—right?"

"I'm not unreasonable about these things," said Sniff. "I know what The Five can do on any given day. And by the way, I told you that I already have my Dream Machine. You weren't listening, apparently."

"Of course, you mean something in a dream, like the one I told you I had, yes?" said Stub. "And not a *real* machine?"

"No," said Sniff. "you're wrong. This isn't fantasy land. This is The Woods."

Stub was dumbfounded, wordless. He looked at Sniff for a moment, with his eyes wide open, then spoke: "When do you think The Kingdom of Sharing will be official?"

"It'll take about five hundred more birds, a thousand more butterflies, a hundred more squirrels, and a whole lot of moles," said Sniff.

"Moles?" said Stub, suddenly feeling currents of fear rising in his legs and torso.

"Yes, moles," said Sniff, "even if moles are hard to get at because you spend so much of your time underground."

"But why moles?" asked Stub, his voice tightening.

"Because they're no use to me anymore," said Sniff. "Take you, for instance. All you are is a dreamer, and there's no room in The Woods for dreamers and po-ets."

"But I give you ideas from my dreams," said Stub. "You have *used* my dreams."

"You really *are* a dreamer, aren't you?" said Sniff. "Those ideas and dreams were all mine in the first place. They belonged to me because I'm a leader who will soon be the leader of The Woods."

"But we're friends—aren't we friends?" said Stub.

"I don't need you anymore, and that's final," said Sniff, who turned around abruptly and left.

All Stub could do was drop underground, feeling very confused and very scared.

33: Stub Rats on Sniff

The first thing the next day, Stub set out to find Wing. Finally, there he was, on a limb of an ash tree that Stub knew he frequented in the morning. Knowing already that Wing and Sniff were enemies, Stub didn't need to waste a lot of words on preliminaries, when he called out:

"Listen, Wing," he said, "I want to tell you something about Sniff."

"That's a good subject," said Wing, "or should I say, like Frog, a good/bad subject? What do you have to say about your friend?"

"He's not my friend anymore if he ever was," said Stub.

"He's not your friend?" said Wing.

"No. I want to tell you about Sniff's lies," said Stub.

"Another good/bad subject," said Wing.

"He's got a secret tunnel under The Maze, and he uses it for his exhibition runs. I know it's true because I was in on the digging."

"A tunnel under The Maze?" said Wing, feigning surprise with wide-open eyes. "That mazes me."

"Yes," said Stub, "he's got two trap doors inside The Hard Way—one close to The Beginning, and one close to The End. That's how he gets in and then gets out."

"That's good information," said Wing. "But why do you bring it to me?"

"Because he's the worst liar in the history of The Woods," said Stub, "and he's got to be stopped, and you're an animal who can do something about it."

"What other lies by Sniff are you referring to?" asked Wing.

"Lots of other lies," said Stub. "First, there's the letters. You know, the letters to Owl by all of the animals who send him money for his autograph? You know, the ones that Sniff tells that he's gonna have the letters framed and then hung up on The Big Limb after Owl retires?"

"Yes?" said Wing.

"You won't be seeing any letters on The Big Limb," said Stub. "That's a lie."

"How so?" said Wing.

"Because he makes fake money out of those letters," said Stub.

"Fake money?" said, Wing.

"That's right," said Stub. "At night, when Owl's out hunting, he has The Five cut up the letters into the exact size of paper money. And since owls can't see things close up, he gives the fake money to Owl, and he thinks it's real money."

"And Sniff keeps the real money for himself?" said Wing.

"Most of the paper money, anyway," said Stub. "Owl gets the coins and Sniff gets most of the rest of the autograph money."

"I see," said Wing. "At least Owl gets to keep *some* money for his retirement. But how do you know this?"

"I know it because I've been there in The Hole and I've seen it," said Stub. "The Five just drop the real money down a hole inside The Hole, into Sniff's big nest."

"Keep talking," said Wing.

"And not only that," Stub went on. "Sniff also steals my dreams."

"Steals your dreams?" said Wing.

"That's right," said Stub. "The Maze and the tunnel and the Dream Machine. All three of them came out of my dreams, and he stole them, and got all the credit."

"So he's also a dream poacher," said Wing. "What else can you tell me?"

"Okay," said Stub. "Here's another way he cheated. Before the building of The Hard Way and the tunnel, he had a couple of vigilantes hiding inside The Easy Way. When any animal who was not a rat was running too fast, they would stick out a leg and trip them up, and that would make their time slower. Especially Claws, because he's getting so fast. Anyway, that's another way Sniff's been cheating. There's no vigilantes anymore because he can just run through the tunnel."

"Keep going," said Wing.

"Have you heard of The Committee on Population?" said Stub.

"No," said Wing.

"Five nights a week, in his nest, he gets together with the members of the committee. Every week the committee has new members, all females, usually at least six of them. Can you guess what's going on in those meetings?"

"They're having deep discussions on population?" said Wing.

"Not at all," said Stub. "Whenever you see a lot of little rats running around, you can bet that most of them come from those meetings."

"How do you know this is going on?" said Wing.

"I can hear them, and mostly feel the vibrations through the walls," said Stub.

"I'm not mazed nearly as much by that revelation," said Wing.

"Not only that," said Stub, "but Sniff told me he didn't need a Dream Machine because he's already got one."

"He's already got one?" said Wing.

"He says his Dream Machine is The Word. Like when he gives commands to The Five, and they go out and kill animals, which he calls Old World animals. He gives the orders, and The Five do the bloody work of killing them off. And he says he wouldn't kill Fox, even though he tells all of us that he wants to kill him, at every Appearance. He said he wants to keep Fox around because he needs him to keep the animals scared."

"I'm still listening," said Wing.

"He says he even wants to have us moles killed off too," said Stub. "He told me that to my face."

"And what did you say when he told you that?" asked Wing.

"I was shocked," said Stub. "I've been working for Sniff for a long time. I've always been doing a good job and he knows it."

"But why are you telling me all of these things?" asked Wing.

"Because you're Sniff's biggest enemy, besides Fox," said Stub. "Maybe you can do something to stop him. If somebody doesn't stop him, he'll kill off all of the animals except the rats."

"I very much appreciate all of this information," said Wing.

"But what do you plan to do about it?" asked Stub.

"There is one thing *you* can do to help out," said Wing.

"And what's that?" said Stub.

"You can tell as many moles as possible not to vote for Sniff in the election," said Wing.

"I'll do that," said Stub. "And I said all these things I'm telling you to a good friend. We're both members of the ARL."

"The ARL?" said Wing.

"The Anti-Rules League," said Stub. "It's a very active group, I can tell you."

"Good," said Wing. "That's very good. We'll need all the help we can get. I'm sure we'll be talking more about this Sniff matter soon, and certainly agree to collaborate."

"For sure," said Stub. "Just let me know what else I can do." Stub paused, dropped his look, then looked up again, very intently, at Wing. "If Sniff knew I told you what I just told you," he said, "he'd have me killed."

"I understand," said Wing. "I certainly won't let our conversation get back to him. And thanks again for the information. I think it could turn out to be very useful—not only to you and me but to all of us in The Woods."

The two thanked each other, the conversation was over, so Wing flew up and away just as Stub dropped back down into his tunnel.

34: Enter the Serpent

As he was waiting on a low branch for Snake to appear in his bushy locale, where he had observed him many times, Wing was feeling anxious. He was recalling what he'd told Butterfly at the end of their conversation about her talk with The Crow: that it was his turn to talk to Snake. At the very second the words came out of his beak, he had all but decided (secretly) to hire Snake not to *scare* Sniff (as they'd just agreed to do), but to *kill* him. But now, at this moment, looking down at the bushes, he had a change of heart, knowing that even if their plan failed in the end—and it was certainly a bold plan—he wouldn't be able to live with the betrayal of his best friend.

Finally, Snake emerged from under a bush.

"Can we talk?" said Wing, flapping a wing a little to get Snake's attention.

"ABOUT WHAT?" said Snake, looking up, now upright, very tall, shaped like an S, hip-less.

"I'd like to talk to you about a certain animal around here," said Wing.

"WHICH ONE?" said Snake.

"A rat named Sniff," said Wing. "Have you heard of him?"

"YEAH, I KNOW WHO HE IS," said Snake. "SO, YOU KNOW WHAT I AM?"

"You're a rat snake," said Wing.

"YOU BETTER BELIEVE IT," said Snake.

"I'm wondering if you could be hired to scare this rat into quitting his wicked ways."

"YOU MEAN YOU JUST WANT HIM SCARED BUT NOT KILLED?"

"Just scared, yes," said Wing.

"THAT WON'T BE EASY FOR A RAT SNAKE," said Snake. "THIS IS HOW WE KEEP ALIVE—SQUEEZ'N AND THEN EAT'N RATS, NOT SCAR'N 'EM."

"Even if the money is right?" said Wing.

"WHAT KIND'A MONEY YOU TALK'N ABOUT?"

"Ten dollars?" said Wing.

"MAKE IT FIFTEEN?" said Snake.

"Twelve and a half?" said Wing.

"OKAY," Said Snake. "WHAT'S YOUR PLAN?"

"Are you familiar with The Maze?" said Wing.

"THAT'S THE THING WITH WALLS THAT'S CLOSE TO THE OAK," said Snake, "WITH ALL THE TWISTS AND TURNS AND DEAD-ENDS INSIDE IT?"

"That's right," said Wing.

"KEEP TALK'N," said Snake.

"Sniff runs through a tunnel under The Maze instead of taking the regular maze route," said Wing. "And he'll be using that tunnel for his exhibition run on Friday evening—it'll be Owl's last Appearance."

"WAIT A MINUTE. WHY WOULD HE BE RUNNING THROUGH A TUNNEL UNDER THE MAZE?" said Snake.

"Because he's a cheater and that's the only way he can set the record," said Wing. "Now a mole named Stub will meet you at The Maze—"

"A MOLE!" said Snake.

"Yes, he'll help you," said Wing.

"I PUT THE BIG SQUEEZE ON MORE THAN A FEW MOLES IN MY DAY, I CAN TELL YA THAT," said Snake.

"No, no, Stub is a friend, and you'll need his help," said Wing, gesturing in a friendly way. "He'll let you into The Maze through a trapdoor. You can situate yourself so that you're facing the entrance—and then when Sniff makes his run in front of a big crowd at Owl's last Appearance, and comes through, he'll meet you head-to-head, and of course, turn around and run the other way."

"OH, I GUARANTEE HE'LL BE GOING THE OPPOSITE WAY THE SECOND HE GETS A GLIMPSE OF ME," said Snake.

"That's exactly the plan," said Wing. "And then when Sniff comes back out the same way he went into that tunnel, Stub will let you out the other trapdoor, near the entrance. I'll be up there on The Big Limb, so I can let the crowd know what they've just witnessed with their own eyes—thanks to you—that Sniff is nothing but a low-life con-rat."

"SOUNDS WORKABLE," said Snake. "WHEN DO YOU WANT ME TO, AS YOU SAY, SITUATE MYSELF IN THAT TUNNEL?"

"Okay," said Wing. "Stub will meet you at The Maze very early Friday morning—in fact, let's make it four a.m."

"YOU WANT ME LAY'N IN THAT TUNNEL FOR ALL THOSE HOURS BEFORE THAT RAT COMES THROUGH?" said Snake.

"It'll be a bit of a wait," said Wing. "But we have to make sure you're not discovered."

"MAKE IT FIFTEEN BUCKS, THEN," said Snake. "THAT'S A LONG TIME TO GO WITHOUT A MEAL."

"Fifteen it'll be," said Wing.

"I WANT YOU TO KNOW THAT I'LL BE MIGHTY HUNGRY BY SIX O'CLOCK," said Snake.

"Now of course you know you won't be eating that rat," said Wing.

"I GOT IT," said Snake. "JUST SCARE HIM—BUT OH, I CAN TELL YOU, IT WON'T BE EASY! AND THEN I GOTTA WORK WITH A MOLE."

"I understand," said Wing.

"BEFORE I GO, HOW ABOUT AN ADVANCE?" said Snake.

"No problem," said Wing. "In fact, I might as well let you have the full fifteen," and he gave Snake the money.

"I'LL CATCH YOU LATER," said Snake, turning around and suddenly—not slithering away, not disguising himself in the weeds, but upright, like a tall S—he was gone.

For at least an hour in the air, Snake's word *catch* kept an alarming grip on Wing's mind.

35: New Woods' Election Notice

By Wednesday, a notice in big red letters and with the heading, "New Woods' Election Notice," was attached to hundreds of trees:

DEAR FELLOW NEW WOODSIAN OF THE KINGDOM OF SHARING:

Due to his great experience and wisdom, Owl has designated Sniff to be his personal choice for the New Leader of the New Woods.

Any opinions that differ from Owl's wise choice may be discussed with The Five, before the election on Friday, which will take place at Sniff's Exhibition Run as well as Owl's last Appearance, beginning at 6 p.m. It is sincerely hoped and assumed that you fully understand and fully appreciate Owl's wise selection of Sniff as The Distinguished New Leader of The Kingdom of Sharing.

Yours Truly,
The Five, Co-Rats of the Committee on the New Woods Election (CNWE)

36: Owl's Last Appearance; the Election

Not only were a great many four-legged animals present at Owl's final Appearance, such as rats, minks, a surprisingly large turnout of moles, along with voles, chipmunks and weasels; there were also many squirrels, and many birds, such as sparrows, hawks, owls, doves, grackles, ducks and woodpeckers. And more than that: hovering in the sky over the ground crowd were two black clouds of birds—a huge flock of crows, and a smaller flock of blackbirds. Wing and Number Two were standing on The Big Limb, each holding a microphone. Sniff was inside The Hole with Owl. Butterfly was perched on a branch. Claws—the only other candidate for leader besides Sniff—was inside the crowd on the ground, not far from the four (of The Five). Frog was also present, along with the Possums, Spider, and Number Three. Stub was hiding inside The Maze, having guided Snake inside many hours earlier.

To start the Appearance, Number Two raised his microphone and spoke: "My fellow animals of The Woods, now that Owl will no longer be living in The Oak, this evening's collection will be going to what Sniff believes is another great cause: The Oak Restoration

Fund." The Four moved about in the crowd with their cups, accepting money with gracious smiles.

The noise of singing and yelling and squawking and talking and stamping became quite loud by the time Owl stepped belatedly out of The Hole. He accepted the microphone from Number Two, glanced at Wing, then waited for the crowd to settle down. He looked down and spoke, more terse than ever.

"Animals of the Woods, Yoooooooooo have been so kind to me, yoooooooooo have been so dooooooooooootiful, yoooooooooo have been so kind to me, yoooooooooooo have been so dooooooooooiful. It is yoooooooooo."

Owl gave the microphone back to Number Two, waved to the crowd, and his waving became a signal to a couple of young, stout-looking owls, who stepped out of The Hole, each carrying a large, heavy bag. They stood there for several seconds, acknowledging the crowd, and then all three owls, with perfect timing together, dropped off The Big Limb and swooped down, circled the crowd twice, and vanished into the trees.

More applause came—sincere, grateful applause. Sniff stepped out of The Hole as the noise was dying down. He took the microphone from Number Two, then waved to the applauding animals below him, smiling proudly, as if, as usual, accepting the applause as his own.

"Animals of the Woods," he said, "the Great Owl is gone. It is time for the New Woods." He dropped the microphone to his side, as if to encourage the crowd noise to begin again, and it did, this time with more cheering and yelling. Many of the perching birds left their perches and flew around, which frightened the rabbits, who bolted to safety; several raccoons climbed a tree, some squirrels climbed another one. The noise went on and on then finally waned, and stopped. Then Sniff said, "Animals of The Woods, have you forgotten my exhibition run?"

"Noooooo!" yelled The Four together, "Noooooo!" Sniff smiled and went on: "Okay," he said, "as I told you last week, I intend to set a new maze record this evening, and all of you will be the lucky witnesses." Sniff gave the microphone to Number Two, climbed down to the ground, and walked to The Beginning. The crowd was now turned around and watching. He signaled up to the starter, set his body for a dramatic-looking start, and when he heard the word "Go!" disappeared inside the entrance.

Ten seconds went by . . . fifteen seconds . . . twenty-five . . . and all at once Sniff came stumbling at his top-speed-clumsy gait back out of the entrance. He stopped, and looked, his face whitish, at the astonished crowd, his eyes narrowed, his ears flattened. He took a few seconds to compose himself, shook his head, then climbed back up on The Big Limb. Now there were three standing in a row: Sniff on one side, Number Two in the middle, and Wing, the biggest of the three, on the other end. Sniff took the microphone from Number Two. "Animals of the Woods," he said. "One of the laws of The Maze (his speech at first was slightly shaky) has just been violated—I mean broken, and it has prevented me from completing my exhibition run." The crowd surged, many looked dumbfounded. Several animals were heard to say "What happened?" Sniff spoke again: "I'll tell you exactly what happened. The 'no snakes' rule—I mean the 'no snakes' *law* has been broken because a snake got inside The Hard Way and was blocking my record run."

Just as Sniff finished his sentence, Snake began to emerge from the tunnel—all of the animals watching him, and many moving back quickly to form a wide lane— growing gradually more upright and S-shaped, drawing his long body through the entrance and, finally, all the way out. Dusty all over his body, he stopped, and began to shake and writhe.

"Oh, look," said a weasel, "it's Snake."

"Yes," said another weasel, "it's him alright."

"There he is," said Sniff, pointing at Snake. "He's the one that broke the law of The Maze." Several rabbits ran away, many other animals uttered words of astonishment and fear.

Wing put his microphone to his beak and spoke up. "My fellow animals," he said, waving his free wing to get their attention: "let me clear up any confusion about what has just happened, what you have just witnessed. First of all, notice that Snake is very dusty, as if he's just come out of a place that's not actually the inside of The Maze itself, I mean, The Hard Way, but from a much dustier, darker place, with walls made out of dirt. In fact, he was not *in* The Hard Way at all—as Sniff said—but in a secret *tunnel* below The Hard Way, a *tunnel* that Sniff—yes, Sniff—had built for himself. You all remember recently when The Maze was closed for repairs. That was when the tunnel was built. The tunnel has two trapdoors, one near the entrance and one near the exit, to let Sniff into it and to let him out of it." Wing paused a moment.

"A tunnel?" said one of the chipmunks. "Why would he want a tunnel?"

"He's a liar," said a mink.

"Who's a liar?" said an old squirrel.

"Wing," said another mink. "What does he know?"

"Wait a minute," said a young squirrel. "Sniff cheated. That's how he set the record."

"Sniff is still the champion," said a chipmunk.

Wing went on: "Animals of The Woods, listen to me: the reason Sniff had a tunnel built was to be able to set a record by running in a straight line instead of having to take all of those zig-zag left and right turns by running *through* The Maze—in other words, Sniff cheated." Wing paused once more, giving the crowd more time to respond:

"I don't believe it," said a rabbit. "Wing is a liar."

"I believe it," said a mole close by. "Sniff broke the rule that says 'no cheating.'"

Wing spoke again, "What do you have to say now, Sniff? Am I lying?"

"Excuse me," said Sniff, sniffing. "You're talking about the repair tunnel. The snake was not in the repair tunnel. Why would he be in the repair tunnel? He was in the Hard Way, breaking the law."

"Alright," said Wing, "would you care to prove it to all of us? Would you like to prove that you are right and I am wrong?"

"You are wrong," said Sniff, looking at the crowd, and sniffing.

"Alright," said Wing. "Why don't you go back down there and do your exhibition run *inside* The Hard Way, where you *said* you were, and we can all be witnesses to your record run. Or, if you prefer to use the tunnel again, it's empty now. There's the snake (Wing pointed at Snake, who moved away into the trees)—you can see that he's no longer down inside that dusty place."

Sniff turned silent for several seconds, then raised his microphone and spoke: "My fellow animals of The Woods, all this amounts to is a big misunderstanding. I can clear it all up easily, and I will do that later—but let me ask you all, right now: why are we here this evening?" Some in the crowd were still cheering him, and some were booing. Many were silent, just looking around vaguely, or at one another.

"Listen, all of you," Sniff yelled out, "Why are we here?" and looked down at The Four.

"To vote!" The Four shouted together. "To Vote!"

"We're here," said Sniff, "to elect the new leader of The Woods, and so I must now allow our two announcers to proceed." He gave the microphone back to Number Two and took a couple of steps away from him.

Again, there was some booing and cheering and talking. A squirrel said, "Sniff's a cheater." Another squirrel said, "yeah, but he's still the champion of The Maze."

Number Two lifted his microphone: "We have two candidates for leadership of The Woods," he said. "Sniff and Claws. Claws will need to come up here on The Big Limb, for the vote." Claws immediately climbed up on The Big Limb and stood next to Sniff, who then grabbed the microphone from Number Two: "My fellow animals," he said, waving his free paw, "I want you to know that—"

"Excuse me," said Wing, breaking in, "but it's not proper protocol for you to say anything right now. (At that moment Wing was aware of hating a phrase that had just come out of his beak: *proper protocol.*) You, Sniff, just like Claws, must keep quiet during the voting." There was a brief burst of applause from some in the crowd.

"So now," said Number Two, taking the microphone back from Sniff and speaking again, "we have two candidates, Sniff and Claws, and two election officials—me and Wing. I will ask for ayes for Sniff, and Wing will ask for ayes for Claws." Number Two held up a coin for all of the animals to see. "Wing," he said, "you call heads or tails. Whoever wins can choose to have his vote for his candidate first, or second."

"Heads," said Wing. Number Two flipped the coin and caught it in his extended paw. "It's heads," he said, showing it to Sniff, then to Claws. "Wing chooses to go first or second," said Number Two. "Which is it?"

"I'll go second," said Wing.

"Okay," said Number Two. "Listen up, animals of The Woods," he said in his resonant, articulate voice, standing up straight and holding his head high. "All those in favor of Sniff, for the leader of The Woods, indicate by saying *aye.*"

The ayes began with The Four, who were also stamping and waving, and others joined in with their ayes—all of the rest of the rats as well, and other four-legged animals, and some perched and flying birds. The ayes increased in number—kept on increasing until they reached a peak, then began, slowly, to diminish. Number Two kept raising his paw and gesturing for more votes, which kept coming for a couple of moments more, and then finally, little by little, stopped.

Now all animals turned to Wing. He put his microphone to his beak, raised his head and his free wing high: "Animals of the Woods," he announced loudly in his microphone, "all those in favor of Claws, for the leader of The Woods, indicate by saying *aye*."

The response was immediate and huge, an outburst of ayes from birds and frogs and toads and moles and voles and minks and skunks and chipmunks and opossums. Many butterflies, that couldn't be heard, were fluttering excitedly over and under The Big Limb. The two flocks of birds above the crowd were moving excitedly up and down and sideways and over and under, now flattening out, now swelling into thick black masses, the sound of their ayes increasing in number and volume—those from the raucous crows being dominant—and finally the noise became an immense sound, the individual ayes blending into one protracted *ayyyyyyyyyyyyyye*. Just as a crescendo was reached and it was becoming clearer and clearer that the long-lasting sounds for Claws had made him the winner, Sniff and Number Two climbed down to the ground, ducking their heads as if escaping a hail storm, and, accompanied by the other four of The Five, scrambled away into the shadows of trees.

Wing turned and looked at Claws, who was beaming and swishing his tail. Wing gave him the microphone. Claws looked down at the cheering crowd, then up at the friendly, hovering flocks of crows and blackbirds. When the animals knew he was about to speak, they turned silent. "Thank you," Claws said, "Thank you very much."

The cheering began again, then died down. "Thank you," he said once more, and gave the microphone back to Wing, who set it down on the limb, and flew away, joining Butterfly in the air—leaving Claws by himself, still beaming, and acknowledging the crowd.

"Look at him," said a rabbit. "He's a true champion."

"And he's a squirrel of few words," said a chipmunk. "Just like Owl."

"But he's a poet," said a mole, "so I think he'll have a lot more to say later on."

The Appearance was over, and all of the animals dispersed and went home.

37: Coda: At the Edge of The Meadow

A half-hour after the election, Butterfly and Wing were talking on a high branch of an elm, at the edge of The Meadow.

"I didn't think those ayes for Claws would ever stop," said Wing.

"Especially from all of those crows," said Butterfly.

"Do you think The Crow had something to do with so many crows showing up?" said Wing.

"Yes, I do," said Butterfly. "I forgot to tell you that he mentioned the election after our talk, but I assumed at the time that he was just curious. I didn't express my feelings about Sniff directly to him, but he may have sensed them."

"I've heard that crows are extremely sensitive to voice tones," said Wing. "And not only that but they also tend to hold grudges for a long time. Who knows—maybe he's carrying a grudge against Sniff for something that happened when he used to live in The Woods?"

"Perhaps," said Butterfly. "and no doubt he still knows a lot of crows in The Woods. He didn't strike me as one who easily tolerates nefarious behavior. I'm sure now that he wanted to help us. How else can you explain all those wonderful, deafening ayes raining down from the sky?"

"I was somewhat surprised at how many votes Sniff actually got," said Wing. "Every single animal could see with its own eyes that he cheated."

"I was surprised too," said Butterfly. "And you explained the cheating to the crowd very clearly. That was double proof, wasn't it?"

"Yes it was," said Wing. "But I'm convinced that facts and the truth can never compete with belief."

"In any case," said Butterfly, "it is true that all of those votes for Claws came from individuals. Right? The *I* of the *I-We*?"

"Of course," said Wing, "So what are you getting at?"

"I'm just remembering you saying that individuals always come first," said Butterfly.

"Yes, I remember saying it," said Wing.

"And do you still believe that we're more selfish than unselfish?" said Butterfly.

"I'll probably be re-thinking that opinion," said Wing. "It *is* interesting that it was Sniff's philosophy of togetherness and group harmony that enabled Claws to win the election. Let's say that every vote was for the *I* and for the *We* at the same time. Frog might call it a happy convergence of opposites."

"That makes some sense," said Butterfly.

"I suppose you would say that the election proved that there's a universal moral sense," said Wing.

"Yes," said Butterfly, "I do think so."

"Maybe it's true for most animals," said Wing, "if not every single one. So how would you sum up what the election today at The Oak means to you?"

"I would say it means that whenever a very large group of animals agree to say aye together, as one, in order to improve life in The Woods," said Butterfly, "the result tends to be in favor of justice, and goodness."

"I hope you're right," said Wing. "Regarding Sniff, he won't be leaving us until he's circled back and picked up his money, if he hasn't already done it. And if he doesn't come back someday to threaten our existence, other Sniffs will show up in his place. There's plenty of Sniffs out there. We've all got to stay vigilant."

"Vigilance is a necessity in The Woods," said Butterfly.

"I wonder if you'd agree with me," said Wing, "that what happened today also means that the tradition established by Owl will live on, just as another important tradition is about to begin. And this new one will be more inclusive and tolerant—that is, it will accommodate a greater variety of animals, and ways of living."

"I agree," said Butterfly. "I like your summary."

"And I would add only one more thing that's missing from the mix—a reminder," said Wing.

Butterfly's delicate wings began to flutter. "And what's that?" she said.

"You owe me seven and a half dollars for my talk with Snake," said Wing.

"Oh, in my excitement I forgot!" said Butterfly. "I'll certainly have it the next time we meet."

"Let's make it soon," said Wing, and the two friends had a laugh together, said goodbye, then flew off in their preferred directions.